DANCING THROUGH LIFE
BOOK TWELVE

PRIMA *Ballerina*

PATRICIA M. ROBERTSON

Prima Ballerina

Patricia M. Robertson

Ashley handed her driver's license and credit card to the counter person at Avis rental cars. It had already been a long day and it wasn't over. Tired from the afternoon performance and flight from New York, all Ashley wanted was to be back home in her apartment, icing her feet with a bag of frozen peas, sipping wine and preparing to sleep in her cozy bed covered by her down comforter. Instead, here she was, waiting for a rental car in Detroit. The sun was setting by the time her flight arrived at Metro Airport. She had another hour of driving ahead of her. Why had she opted for this flight instead of waiting till tomorrow?

"New York," the woman muttered.

"Yes, is that a problem?" Ashley balanced the two sets of luggage she had managed to drag from the luggage carousel, then on to the shuttle bus for a ride to the rental place. What a pain. Was there something wrong with having a New York driver's license? She had traveled abroad and had less trouble going through customs than she was having getting a rental car. Of course, those previous times she had been travelling with her dance company. The company took care of all the arrangements. All she had to do was pack her bag, make sure she had her passport, and show up on time to be picked up and transported to the airport.

No need for a rental car. No need for a car – period – living in New York City. She used cabs and the subway for all of her transportation needs. And for those excursions out of the city, to upstate New York and the Catskills, or for a weekend in Vermont, cars were taken care of by her current beau. No need to worry herself with driving.

It had been years since she was behind the wheel of a car.

The woman ignored her question. "Do you have proof of insurance? If you don't have insurance you will have to purchase ours."

"Of course, I don't have insurance. I don't own a car. Why would I have insurance?"

"You'll need to sign up for insurance. Here are the options ..." The woman peered at her over her glasses, tapping her fingers while Ashley read over the paperwork.

"If you need more time, step aside so I can help the next customer."

Why hadn't Michael told her about this? "No, just give me what I need to get on the road."

"We can't let just anybody drive away in one of our cars."

"Apparently you don't know who I am." Oh, that's right. She was no longer in New York.

"Then why do you need a rental? Last I checked, there was no limo waiting to pick you up."

She had her there. Ashley looked at the woman's nametag. Shirley. Ashley signed up for what appeared to be the basic insurance and handed Shirley her credit card. "Look, Shirley, just do whatever you have to do to get me on the road."

Shirley looked over the papers, charged her credit card and handed her a set of keys with a map showing where her rental car was located.

Ashley looked at the key fob that had been placed in her hand. How hard could it be? "Where's the key?" Ashley stared at the fob. There was no key that she could tell.

"It's keyless entry. You have driven cars with push button ignitions, haven't you?" Shirley looked over her glasses at Ashley again, a sneer formed on her lips and reverberated in the question.

How dare she? Did she know who she was talking to? She was Ashley Reese, prima ballerina with one of New York's premiere ballet companies, affectionately referred to as "The Company" by its dancers.

"When you're close enough to the car, the door unlocks automatically. You push in the ignition to start. All you have to do is have the fob in the car to drive."

"Sure. Of course." Ashley had no idea. But there was no way she was going to let this woman know that. Had cars changed that much since she had last driven one?

"Next," Shirley dismissed her.

Now all she had to do was find the car. How hard could that be? She looked at the map. It showed her where her car was, but not how to get to the parking lot. No way she was going to ask Shirley how to get there. She looked for someone to ask, saw the couple that had been behind her at the counter and followed them. No problem.

Her dad had offered to pick her up at the airport. He would have done it in a heartbeat, but she would have none of that.

"And appear like a helpless school girl who can't even drive a car?" she had responded. "And then be dependent on others and their cars the whole time I'm there?"

"Ava and I'd be happy to drive you. Gives us more time with you. Or you could drive one of our cars."

"Dad, I've been living on my own in New York for fifteen years. I think I can manage to find my way home from the airport."

"It's not that I think you can't. It's just ... you're so grown-up. I have so few opportunities to treat you like a daughter. Humor me. Let me do this." Ashley heard the kindness in his voice. It was almost enough to get her to give in. What would it hurt?

But Ashley prevailed as she did most times, fighting the urge to give in to her dad. How hard could it be? It's like riding a bike, right? Once you know how, you never forget.

Maybe that had been a mistake.

Learning to drive hadn't been a high priority back in high school. She had taken a drivers' training course and spent the required amount of time using her learner's permit, driving with another licensed driver in the car, until she got her license. Once acquired, it no longer seemed that important. After that, her focus had been on getting out of Cascade Falls as quickly as possible. She drove when she was home on breaks, but since she started dancing with The Company ten years ago, she hadn't been home. That was a long time to go without driving. She kept her license up-to-date as an ID.

Ashley found the car, threw her suitcases in the back seat, then sat down behind the wheel and stared at the dashboard. Her right foot searched for pedals. Yes, the gas and the brake were in the same place she remembered. There was a button where she had expected to find the ignition. She pushed the button in and was surprised as the car came to life. Nothing to it.

As she turned on the navigation on her phone, her parents' address popped up. All she had to do was get on I-94 going west and she'd be home before she knew it. She adjusted the mirrors, put the car in reverse, backed out and was on her way.

Bright lights of moving cars startled her as she pulled out of the parking area. Where had all these vehicles come from? She eased the car into the right lane only to be told to cross three lanes of traffic and stay to the left by the automated voice. How was she going to cross three lanes of traffic?

Horns blared as she slowed down to move into the next lane, stopping traffic behind her and cutting off traffic in the lanes. She made it into the far lane and thought she was home free — but then she missed an exit and ended up circling the airport.

Good practice, she told herself as she circled through the airport twice before finding I-94. She let out a sigh of relief when she saw the entrance ramp for I-94 West to Chicago. Finally. She veered right onto the ramp and onto I-94 where a surge of truck traffic blocked her from merging onto the highway. She remained in the merging lane while the trucks zoomed by, rattling her Ford Fiesta. "Merge left onto I-94 West," the voice of her navigation system kept repeating. She still had room in her lane, Ashley thought as she crawled along looking for her opening, until she saw that the entrance lane had turned into an exit lane. She had no option but to exit.

"Recalculating, recalculating," the voice repeated. Ashley knew that message from her three trips around the airport. She took a right after the exit, staring into the darkness for road signs to let her know where she was.

"Make a U-turn at the first opportunity," the voice stated.

Make a U-turn? Where was she going to do that?

Ashley turned down a road lined with hotels, pulled into the drive of the closest one and took a deep breath as she assessed the situation. Maybe she should get a room and continue home tomorrow in daylight? But no. She was Ashley Reese, prima ballerina. She had this.

She went back the way she had come in, turned left on the road and saw the entrance ramp. This time traffic had cleared enough so she was able to get into the lane. Easy! She was on her way.

The prodigal daughter would soon be home.

Chapter 2

Once she got clear of the Detroit/Ann Arbor area, Ashley gave the voice command to call home.

"Hey, Dad. I'm on my way. Should be there in a half an hour or so."

"Drive carefully. We'll be waiting for you."

Ashley smiled at the sound of her dad's voice coming over the speaker on the phone. She was almost looking forward to this.

Only her brother's wedding would have gotten her out of New York. He had caught her in a moment of weakness last December, calling her in between performances of *The Nutcracker*. He had been so convincing at the time, wanting to work around her schedule before setting the date for the wedding. Filled with Christmas nostalgia, going home hadn't seemed like such a bad idea. She had agreed on an off-season time in the summer, when the theater was black, meaning they were closed.

Michael, her fiancée, hadn't been much help. She had thought she could count on him to dissuade her from abandoning him, but no. He had insisted she should go.

"Of course, you have to go. It's your brother's wedding. Besides, when am I going to meet this family of yours?"

But two weeks? How could she have agreed to that long. Why couldn't she have just flown in for the wedding and flown back? The two weeks had been at the suggestion of the company's artistic director.

"It will be good for you. You need a break. When was the last time you had a real vacation?"

"You know that as well as I do. The only breaks I have are when we aren't in production. And even then, I have to keep in shape." The life of a young woman, aspiring to be a prima ballerina, did not have a lot of room for distractions. Nor did the life of a prima ballerina. Her only distractions had come in the form of suitors and patrons of the arts. It was part of her role as prima ballerina to cater to patrons so they would continue to fund the company. She only had time for men who understood the demands placed on her as a ballerina. Men who understood ballet came first in her life.

To think, only this afternoon she had been on stage, listening to applause, receiving accolades from adoring fans as she took her bows for her performance in *Giselle*. Ashley listened to the music from the performance through her iPhone, reliving the afternoon. As prima ballerina, she danced all of the coveted roles, like Aurora in *Sleeping Beauty*, their next production. Every Christmas she was the Sugar Plum Fairy in *The Nutcracker*. It was nice to know the roles were hers. She had earned them through hard work and talent. No more inter-company politics and competition — well, less. She couldn't simply rest on her laurels. There was always someone younger coming up the ranks, eager for the opportunity to replace an aging ballerina, just as she had been. She figured she had two or three years left. Maybe more than that, but not much. She was in her prime, but that prime had an expiration date. If not thirty-five, then shortly afterwards. Then what would she do?

Ashley didn't want to think about that. For so many years, all she had thought about was getting to where she was now. Couldn't she just enjoy it? There would be a life after ballet, but what that would be, she had no idea.

She had been whisked away after the performance by her current beau and fiancé, Michael.

"Your adoring fans await you. And so do I," he had said when he entered her dressing room. Tall, dark and handsome. And what's even better, rich. It didn't get much better than that. He was the prince to her Aurora. "We don't have a lot of time. Are you ready?"

"Almost." She ran a brush through her hair, swung her arms around his shoulders and leaned in for a kiss. "Are you sure you can't come with me? Please. Two weeks in Cascade Falls will be unbearable without you."

"We've already discussed this." He kissed her back. "You know I can't be gone for two weeks. I'll join you in time for the wedding. Now we have to get you out of here or you'll miss that flight."

"Would that be so bad?"

Michael was perfect. Or at least her most perfect beau to date. His grandfather was one of the major supporters of The Company. Besides being in line to inherit his grandfather's fortune, he had his grandfather's good taste in music and the arts. And his good taste in women.

He started to escort her out past fans waiting for autographs. Ashley stopped to sign the autographs.

"It's part of being a prima. You have to give the fans what they want," Ashley told him. She didn't tell him how much she loved this aspect of the position. She especially loved the young girls, aspiring ballerinas who came to matinees. She loved being an inspiration to future generations of dancers.

Michael had a limo waiting to get her to the airport.

"If I miss my flight, what would that hurt? It would give me more time with you," Ashley teased as she cuddled next to him during the drive.

"We'll have time. Now you need to spend time with your family. They do know I'm coming later, don't they? And that we're engaged."

"Oh, that. They will. I have to prepare them."

"What do you mean, prepare them?" Michael pulled at a strand of her hair, playfully twirling it around his finger.

"Isn't it enough that I haven't been home for ten years. I can't just surprise them with a fiancé too. Have to give them, and me, some time to adjust to being back."

Michael frowned and pulled away from her. "A minute ago you were begging me to go with you. How would that have worked? You showing up with your fiancé?"

"I guess I wasn't thinking about that. I was only thinking about you and how much I will miss you." Michael accepted her explanation, as she knew he would. She did mean it, she told herself as he wrapped his arm back around her until they pulled up to the airport entrance.

Michael walked her to the TSA check point. Ashley threw her arms around him for another kiss. "You won't forget me while I'm gone."

"How could I? You're unforgettable."

"That I am. Remember that, and this." She leaned in for one more long kiss before going. Ashley smiled to herself as she remembered that kiss.

Yes. Maybe there would be life after ballet, she thought as she pulled off the highway at Cascade Falls.

Chapter 3

The lights were on when she pulled into the driveway of her family home, just as she knew they would be. Her dad and stepmom would wait up for her. Ava would ply her with food. Dad would ask about her flight and tomorrow it would all begin. All the required visits to and from family members, questions about what she was doing, whether she was seeing anyone. Reminders that she wasn't getting any younger. But for tonight, it was good to be home.

"We were beginning to wonder whether you would actually come," her dad said as he hugged her.

"Of course, I was coming," Ashley replied. "I wouldn't let Jacob down."

"Well, that hasn't exactly stopped you in the past."

Oh, here it comes. And she had just gotten in the door. Recriminations about not coming home before now, missing funerals, holidays, and her sister's wedding.

"She's here. That's all that matters." Ava stepped between them and hugged her. "Did you eat on the plane? Can I get you something?"

Ashley smiled. Just how she expected it to be. She left her luggage at the foot of the stairs and joined her parents at the kitchen table where Ava had snacks set out for her. Her dad was finishing off a piece of pie.

"What can I get you? Something to drink?" Ava asked.

"Water would be good."

"You need something more than water."

Ashley picked up a piece of celery and munched on it. "This is plenty."

"At least let me get you a piece of cherry pie. Not as good as your grandma's but that doesn't stop your dad from eating it." Ava pulled the pie off the counter and held a knife to it, preparing to cut a large slice.

"Just a sliver." Ashley stopped her until Ava cut a piece suitably small enough and served it to her. Ashley smiled and took a bite. She enjoyed being waited on. "This is fabulous."

Ava laughed. "It's hardly fabulous, but I'm glad you like it."

"It's fabulous. Being home is fabulous. Everything about it."

"Remember that after a week of being home. Cascade Falls is a far cry from New York." Ava sat down across from her. "So, tell us, what's been happening in your life?"

"Not much to say." Ashley picked at her pie as she wondered — was it too soon to say something about Michael? "Dancing, practice, performances. That's pretty much my life. I just finished *Giselle*. I'll be doing the lead in *Sleeping Beauty* when I get back. We're going on tour to Vienna. Have to give the audience what they want. But we are doing a new work in the fall. A modern ballet."

"Sounds wonderful. Maybe we can go to New York to see it." Ava looked across the table at her dad.

"That's up to you. You're the one who plans these trips. I just pay the bills." Her dad pushed his plate away. "Hard to believe it's been fifteen years since I first dropped you off at the Detroit airport. You had looked so young, despite your swagger."

"I remember. And I remember how Ava went with me to help me get settled in. New York wasn't exactly your favorite place."

"I learned to deal with it because I had this daughter. If I wanted to see her, I had to go to New York." His corner lip raised in a smile.

"I've come home since then. Remember, those first years I came home for the holidays and while on break over the summer."

"How could I forget? I gained plenty of experience dropping you off and picking you up at the airport. But you haven't been back for ten years." There was no recrimination in his voice. That made it worse.

"I appreciated those times you came to New York." Ashley fought the feelings of regret that were surfacing. She couldn't let those feelings betray her, couldn't let herself admit how much she missed them and her home.

"That was Ava's doings more than mine. She likes planning excursions. Me, not so much. Though I did like watching you in whatever production you were in at the time and going out for dinner."

"You mean you didn't like going shopping with us, carrying our packages, and picking up the tab for lunch?" Ava asked.

"I didn't say that. If it meant spending time with my daughter, I was all for it."

"I know, Dad." Ashley finished off her sliver of pie. "So, what's on the agenda for tomorrow?"

"That's what I was going to ask you," Ava answered.

"You mean you don't have my every waking moment scheduled?"

"Did you want me to?"

"No, not at all." Some things did change, it seemed. Maybe it wouldn't be so bad, being home. What else had changed?

Chapter 4

Ashley woke up in the room she had once shared with her sister, Grace. That was before she claimed the attic for her private hideaway. The attic had since resumed its rightful place as a creepy storage area. She understood. Sorta. Why keep it as an extra bedroom and shrine to her existence when her parents already had more bedrooms than they could fill? Still, the loss irked her as she remembered days spent practicing routines on the hardwood floor, and nights, sneaking out the window to the waiting oak tree. Those had been good times, she had to admit to herself. Her childhood hadn't been the angst-filled melodrama she was fond of creating in her head. The poor, bereft child subject to a wicked stepmother. Her stepmother had been everything but wicked. She had been exceedingly kind and understanding, more than Ashley felt she deserved. She was the wicked stepchild, determined to push away anyone who would dare to deprive her of her rightful lead role in her tragic life.

Ashley was anything but ordinary. Ordinary was for … ordinary people. She was far from that. She had a blessed childhood, a mother who loved her, though she died too soon, a caring father, an equally kind and loving stepmother, along with a host of mother figures in her life: Aunt Kathleen, Grandma Esther, Grandma Mary, Aunt Sara, and all the doting women at the dance studio … No. She couldn't admit that she'd had it so good.

Rather, she was the tragic lead in the drama that was her life. The poor motherless girl who made it, against all odds, as a ballerina in the competitive world of New York City ballet. That had a nice ring to it. Anything less would mean she was — ordinary! She couldn't think of anything worse.

That was the problem with coming home. It exposed the lie her life was built upon. How could she have had such a happy childhood?

Mmmmm. Was that coffee she smelled coming up the stairs from the kitchen? And a hint of cinnamon? Her stepmom's special blend. She usually saved it for exceptional occasions, like holidays. But what could be more exceptional than her return home?

Ashley slipped on the fresh bathrobe her stepmother had set out for her and followed the smell to the kitchen. She paused for a moment to take in the panorama. Sunlight streaming through the windows, promising to be a beautiful Michigan summer day. Ava standing at the stove, flipping French toast. Her dad reading the morning paper. Some things never change, she thought with a smile.

The aroma of coffee, syrup and goodness filled her nose and transported her to an earlier time, when she had been a teen and full of her own self-importance. Every morning it had been the same. The smell of coffee and sound of her dad and stepmom talking before each headed to work. How was it she could have forgotten how wonderful it was to wake up to the sweet smells and soft noises of home? How could she have been so oblivious to what was in front of her?

"Good morning, sleepy-head." Ava turned away from the oven. "Is this how prima ballerinas spend their days off? I was beginning to think you would sleep till noon."

"You can hardly call nine o'clock noon," Ashley countered. "Dad, don't you have to be at work?"

"And miss breakfast with you?" Her dad smiled at her and winked. "What good is owning your own business if you can't come in late now and then?"

"Sit down. Have some French toast. No bacon. That is, if you're still a vegetarian." Ava placed a platter of French toast and bacon on the table.

"No bacon. Even if I weren't still a vegetarian, bacon is not on my list of acceptable foods." Ashley put one piece of French toast on her plate.

"Syrup?" Ava passed her the sticky bottle.

"No syrup. You know I'm on a strict diet."

"But you're on vacation," Ava insisted.

"That's just from performances. There's no vacation from a healthy diet or keeping in shape. Which reminds me. Is the dance studio available for me to practice?"

"Taken care of." Ava handed her a key. "We figured you would want to go there, but can't it wait until tomorrow? I was hoping for some one-on-one time. Maybe go shopping? Once Josie gets here, you'll be busy with wedding activities."

"There'll be time for that. But first I want to establish a routine, as much as possible, for while I'm here."

Her dad picked up his plate, gooey with the syrup that had covered his French toast and the bacon he loved. "Speaking of routine, time for me to get to work. I told everyone I was going to be late. Had to have breakfast with my two best girls. But now, time to go."

Something in her wanted to say, don't go. Sit down. Have another cup of coffee. She knew he would do it for her. But then, what would they say? They had already shared all the normal catching up that was part of coming home last night. What was happening in each other's lives? … The goings-on in Cascade Falls — all the boring, inconsequential, and yet essential details of life in her hometown. She had slipped away to her room last night with the promise of more time to talk, but what was she going to say?

Not that they had been entirely out of touch over the past ten years. There were the occasional phone calls. And Ava, ever the schoolteacher, actually wrote her letters full of news. Who still does that? That kept her informed of the gossip in her hometown and family.

"Remember, Grace and Abel are coming over for dinner tonight," Ava reminded her dad as she stood up and kissed him goodbye. "Don't be late."

"No ma'am." Her dad smiled and winked at her. "Wouldn't think of it."

Ashley finished off her piece of French toast while Ava ran hot water over the sticky dishes in the sink. "You wouldn't happen to have any fruit, do you? And maybe some yogurt?"

"I'll put it on my shopping list. Anything else?"

"Salad stuff, spring mix, tofu. I'll make you a list."

Ava sat back down across from her. "I've forgotten how to cook for a vegetarian. You'll have to remind me."

Not so different from when she had been a kid. Ava had made a valiant effort to accommodate her vegetarianism. She usually came up short. Ashley hadn't appreciated the effort it had taken back then. She appreciated it now.

Ashley sipped her coffee and smiled at her stepmother. "Christmas. Your cinnamon coffee reminds me of Christmas."

"We have a lot of time to make up for. A lot of Christmases missed. Maybe we could have Christmas in June?" Ava pulled out a pad and pen. "Now, tell me everything you want to do while you are here. Any special meals you want me to make. Places you want to go. We'll make a list and plan around the wedding festivities. We might not be able to do all of them, but if we don't at least write them down, the time will be gone before we know it."

Ashley laughed. That was the stepmom she remembered. Every summer she would ask all three of them — Jacob, Grace and her — what they wanted to do during the summer, and had them rate each idea as to most important.

"We won't be able to do everything on your list, but I'll try to make sure we do the top one or two," she said every year until Ashley refused to cooperate anymore, once she'd entered high school. Then Jacob wanted out, wanting only to play basketball and video games. That had left Ava with only Grace until Grace started volunteering at the vet clinic all summer. Even then, Ava tried to organize their lives and coordinate family outings. It was what she did.

"Nothing in particular, everything in general." Ashley put her hand on her stepmom's. "It's enough to be home."

"Is it? I was afraid you would be bored."

"Bored is good. I could use a little boredom. Besides, you think life in New York can't be boring?"

"I couldn't imagine anyone being bored in New York. So much to see and do. So much excitement and activity." Despite her words, her stepmom's eyes seemed sad, tinged with regret as she said them.

"All those things to see and do get old after a while. Besides, that's relegated to the tourists. My life in New York is pretty much the same every day. I get up, have toast and coffee and a piece of fruit, maybe a yogurt, then I go to the studio and practice. Speaking of which —" Ashley started to stand up, but Ava kept hold of her hand.

"I want you to have a good time while you are here, so maybe," Ava paused and squeezed her hand. "Maybe you won't wait so long before visiting again."

That was her cue. She stood up and excused herself. Time to go.

Chapter 5

Ashley pulled into the crowded parking lot behind Joy's Studio of Dance, named by her mom, for her mom. Before she could even try the key to the back door, a group of laughing teens holding coffee cups pushed through the door and past her.

She walked down the narrow entryway and into the main area on the ground floor. The space was filled with small businesses, including a coffee shop and *Froyo* stand. Who'd have thought she'd be able to get espresso and *Froyo* in Cascade Falls, all in the same spot? There was a shop selling art supplies and one with frames for artwork, a yoga studio and ceramic store. While it wasn't exactly bustling, all the spaces were occupied, and small groups of shoppers were in and out.

Her Aunt Kathleen had realized her dream of making the building into a small business hub and center for the arts. All in support of her mom's dance studio.

Ashley took the stairs for the additional work-out, bypassing the elevator. She passed the second floor that held the auditorium and gift shop associated with the dance studio, arriving at the third floor where the office and classrooms were located. She pulled out her keys to unlock the double doors to the dance studio when another group of giggling girls rushed past her. Was this the week for summer dance camp? She had neglected to ask Ava, and Ava had neglected to tell her. Ashley had hoped it would be over so she would be able to practice in solitude.

She opened the door to a frenetic scene of little girls in ponytails, leotards and tutus, running to and from the locker room and the main classroom. If they were in the big classroom, maybe the smaller would be available.

"Ashley!" A brunette with shoulder-length hair and just the hint of crows' feet around her eyes, squeezed her in a massive hug. Aunt Kathleen. Except for the wrinkles and slight frosting of grey, she looked just the way Ashley remembered.

"Why didn't you call me the minute you got in? Chloe, look who's here?" Aunt Kathleen called to another figure from Ashley's past—red-haired, green-eyed Chloe who had taken over the dance studio when Letty had moved to Detroit. Both Chloe and Letty had been key players in getting her where she was.

"You look great." Chloe hugged her as well, then stood back to look at her. "Imagine, a prima ballerina, here in our humble dance studio. You know I tell all my advanced classes about you. Heck, I tell all my classes, even the toddlers. You are something of a local celebrity."

"Second to Jacob, the pro basketball player," Ashley stated.

"Not here. You are first as far as I'm concerned. I'd love to have you talk to my advanced class while you're here. I could still set something up."

"I don't know." Ashley tried to put Chloe off. "I'm here for my brother's wedding. I'm not sure how much free time I'll have."

"Nonsense. You can squeeze in an hour or two to talk to some aspiring ballerinas," Chloe insisted.

Ashley looked to her aunt for help.

"Don't look at me. It would be good for the studio, good business. You know I'm all about the business." Her aunt tipped her head and smiled. "When can we get together for dinner and a sleepover like old times?"

"I won't know when I'll be free until Josie lets me know what's required of being a bridesmaid."

"She can't take all of your time. I'm surprised Ava doesn't already have your calendar set."

"Surprised me too. She actually waited to consult me before drawing up a schedule."

"She must be mellowing in her old age," Aunt Kathleen said.

"Who's mellowing?" Ashley heard the voice of her grandmother, not as steady as she remembered, but unmistakably her. She turned to face the woman she remembered and loved, older, but her smile remained the same, lighting up her face as her eyes sparkled.

"Not you, Grandma." Ashley allowed herself to sink into her grandmother's warm hug. How could she have gone so many years without her grandmother's hugs?

"Let me look at you girl. The spitting image of your mother." Again, that smile, the one that used to reassure her that everything would be okay.

"I thought my mom had brown hair?" That much she remembered. Her mother had had beautiful long light brown hair that she pinned up into a bun, unlike Ashley's blond hair. She remembered watching her mother undo the bun and the hair spilling down her back. Sometimes her mom would let Ashley brush it.

"Color? What difference does color make? A dye job and you're a brunette," Aunt Kathleen said.

"As you should know," Grandma teased.

"Are you implying these locks are anything but my natural color?" Aunt Kathleen raised her eyebrows in mock haughtiness.

"Someday you will realize how nice it is to just let your hair go grey. No more messy dyes. No more chemicals on your head."

"And when I have to start pouring chemicals on my head, I'll stop. Until then, I'm a natural brunette."

Ashley smiled at the two, mother and daughter. She remembered they hadn't always been close, but you wouldn't know it now. Aunt Kathleen's extended adolescence had lasted well into her thirties. She had always loved her aunt's rebellious side and missed it when her aunt "found" God and married a minister. Why was it, the most interesting people she knew didn't believe in God? Once a person accepted a Supreme being, they weren't as much fun.

"I hate to break up the family reunion, but I have a dance studio to keep alive." Chloe interrupted. "Back to you speaking to my advanced class."

"I'm sure Ashley will be happy to — right, Ashley? Your mom would expect it of you," her aunt said.

"Well, when you put it that way," Ashley paused and smiled. "Sure. I'll get back to you once I know my schedule." Who was she to deny her fans, even ones who didn't know her yet?

"How about before then?" Aunt Kathleen wasn't letting it go. "We've got a room full of little girls in Studio One for summer dance camp. Why not show them what you can do?"

Ashley was about to say no, then looked at the three women. How could she say no to them? She needed the practice anyway.

"Okay, just give me twenty minutes to warm up. I'll do something from *Sleeping Beauty*." She would be back in rehearsal for the ballet as soon as she returned. Might as well get some practice before an audience.

"Perfect. I'll arrange it," Chloe said.

Ashley went into Studio Two, removed the light caftan she had thrown over her leotard and started her warm-up. The room was just the way she remembered it. Some things don't change, she thought as she stood next to the barre and stretched her leg onto the railing. She was glad for that.

After stretching and her warmup routine of pliés and relevés, she found the piece from *Sleeping Beauty* ballet she wanted, Aurora's dance at her sixteenth birthday celebration. Even though there were other dancers involved, it was still primarily a solo by Aurora, and it involved music the girls would most likely recognize. She was a little rusty but picked up the choreography quickly. Like bike riding, or driving a car. The steps came back to her as the music played. She could have done *Giselle*, but *Sleeping Beauty* was more appropriate for this age group. They appeared to be between five and eight.

She went through the routine once more, then proceeded to Studio One.

"We have a surprise for you. A real ballerina from New York. Our own Ashley Reese." Chloe introduced her. "Ashley, what are you going to perform for us today?"

"How many of you are familiar with the story *Sleeping Beauty*?"

Most of the girls raised their hands. She looked into their eyes, so bright and innocent and thought, this will be fun! She was delighted at the thought of sharing her love for dance with this small audience.

"It's the story of a beautiful princess, Aurora, who is put into a deep sleep for a hundred years by an evil fairy. This is from the *Sleeping Beauty Ballet* by Tchaikovsky. Princess Aurora is dancing at her sixteenth birthday celebration. Maybe you will recognize the music from the Walt Disney movie," Ashley said as she turned on the music and waited for Aurora's entrance.

As the music played, Ashley lost herself in the dance, in the same room she had seen her mother dance so many times as a child. It was fitting. It wasn't her best performance, or her most sophisticated audience. But it was memorable.

When she finished, she glanced at her aunt Kathleen and grandmother, standing behind the rows of seated girls. Both wiped away tears.

If she expected the same response from the girls, she was mistaken. The joy she had felt at the thought of inspiring another group of dancers quickly disappeared, replaced by shock. How could they not be inspired, if not by her, then the beauty in the music and the dance? The girls dutifully applauded when prompted by their instructor. Stunned, Ashley looked at her aunt and grandmother for help. Aunt Kathleen shrugged and shook her head. Clearly, they were as surprised as she was.

"Of course, in the actual performance there are beautiful costumes, and the hall is filled with other dancers, including the king and queen," Ashley tried to redeem the performance by setting the context for them. Didn't work.

"Can you do anything from *Frozen*?" one girl asked, referring to a Disney movie that was popular for that age group.

"*Frozen*?"

"Yes, you know." The girl started to sing the song "*Let It Go,*" with everyone else chiming in.

"I guess I'm not familiar with that one." Ashley tilted her head and gave a wry smile. "Anyone else?"

"My mother is a better dancer than you," a small voice proclaimed from the back row.

"Shhhh," the teenage instructor admonished the girl.

"That's okay," Ashley told the teen then invited the girl to come forward. She knew how to handle hecklers. A slip of a girl with shoulder-length blonde hair stepped forward. Ashley liked her spunk.

"And you are?" Ashley squatted down to the girl's height.

"Olivia."

"Good to meet you. Is your mother here? I'd like to meet her."

"No. Daddy said she went on a trip."

"Oh." Ashley smiled. "When will she be back?"

"I dunno. Grandma said she's with Jesus. When she's done visiting Jesus, she'll be back."

Ashley felt a sob catch in her throat and tears threaten. She hadn't expected this. Again, she looked over at her aunt and grandmother for help. Olivia was younger than she had been when her mother had died. She looked to be about the age she had been when her mother had first been diagnosed with cancer, around five.

"I'm sure your mother is a very good dancer," Ashley said as Chloe came up and took Olivia's hand.

"Snack time," Chloe said as she led Olivia away to the table in the back of the room, followed by the rest of the class.

"Tough crowd," Aunt Kathleen frowned as she came up to Ashley. "Sorry."

"I didn't expect that," Ashley told her aunt and grandmother. "Did you know?"

"About her mother, yes. But I didn't expect her to blurt out anything like that," Aunt Kathleen said. "Her mom was one of our students, a year or so behind you. Maybe you remember her. Stacey Cochran."

"Oh, yeah. Sure." Ashley lied. She was ashamed to admit how little she had noticed any of the other dancers at the studio. She had been too focused on her own career.

"She was good, though nothing like you." Chloe rejoined the group. "She was one of our instructors. I'm surprised Olivia said anything. Her mom's been gone for over a year. She doesn't talk about her. Doesn't say much about anything. I'll mention it to her father when he picks her up."

Ashley looked at the group of wiggling girls drinking juice pouches. Olivia stood off to the side, pouting, her hands crossed in front of her. Nothing she could do, Ashley told herself. But maybe there was something she could do about the rest of the group, some way to win them over. But what? They were clearly more interested in their snacks than her.

"I need to finish my workout." Ashley excused herself and headed for the door.

"Don't leave without saying goodbye," her aunt instructed.

Ashley shook her head, walked out the door and almost collided with one of the parents. The man stopped and gazed directly into her eyes.

"Ashley?"

She shook her head then looked back into his eyes. The same blue eyes. Same short brown hair, though there was a slight mustache on his upper lip. But there was no mistaking that smile.

"Caleb? I didn't expect to see you here." She was winded, but not from the dance. So many memories attached to that smile. They came rushing at her as if she had seen him only yesterday. She stumbled but was caught by Caleb's strong arm as he steadied her.

"But I expected to see you. Your dad told me you were coming home for the wedding."

"Yes, the wedding of the century." She found herself fumbling for words. For some reason, out of all the people she thought she might run into, she never expected to see Caleb. "I thought you moved away after college. That's what Aunt Kathleen said."

"I did. Then I moved back."

"Whatever for?"

"My mom died. Dad needed help."

"Oh. I'm sorry." How had she not known that? Why hadn't Ava told her? "But you and your dad never got along."

"He's still my dad." Caleb shrugged his shoulders. "Your dad didn't tell you?"

"Why would he?"

"Because I work for him."

Ashley stepped back as she took this in. Not only had her dad not told her Caleb was back in town, but there was also no mention that Caleb was working for him. You'd think he would have said something. Men. And Ava. Why hadn't she said anything in those chatty letters? Not that it mattered. He was just a friend. She had Michael. Still, you never forget your first love.

"What brings you here?" she asked. "You don't exactly strike me as a dance person."

"My daughter." He pointed at the group of girls and waved at one of them. Olivia came running across the room and Caleb opened the classroom door for her. She slipped in next to him, holding his hand and eyeing Ashley with suspicion. Her fingers slipped into her mouth. Clearly no one was going to come between this little girl and her dad.

"Olivia, I'd like you to meet someone," Caleb started.

"We've already met, haven't we, Olivia?" Ashley smiled at the girl.

"Olivia, remember, we've talked about how your fingers don't belong in your mouth." Caleb squatted down next to the girl then looked at Ashley. "I'm sorry. She's been like this since her mother," he paused, his eyes on Olivia, "er … went away."

"I know. She told me her mother was with Jesus."

"She did? Her grandmother told her that."

"And that she's coming back once she's done visiting Jesus."

"Oh, she said that? I didn't know."

"I thought you would like to know." Ashley looked at the pair, another ache stabbing her heart as she remembered her younger self. She stifled a sob.

Caleb stood up. "Hey, it's great seeing you. Maybe we could get together while you're here. Talk about old times?"

"Sure. I'd like that. Call me. Let me give you my number."

"No need. I can get it from your dad. I better get Olivia home." Caleb continued to stare at her as Olivia tugged on his arm. "It was great ... seeing you, that is. I'll call." He finally broke off the gaze, picked up Olivia and carried her to the elevator. Ashley watched as he waited for the elevator to arrive. Olivia turned in his arms, and stared at her over Caleb's shoulder, fingers in her mouth.

Chapter 6

Ashley was prepared to confront her dad over Caleb as soon as he came home, but Grace and her husband, Abel, arrived before him. Grace had her own surprise for Ashley.

"You're pregnant!" Ashley squealed as Grace walked into the house in a loose top over a protruding belly.

"No, I'm just fat. How could you say that?" Grace responded, feigning anger, then burst into laughter. "Yes, I'm pregnant. Isn't it wonderful?"

"It's fantastic! And you look fabulous!" Ashley hugged her sister then hugged the tall, mustached man behind her. "And you must be the daddy-to-be."

"That I am."

"You didn't waste any time."

"When you're my age, there isn't time to waste." Abel's brown eyes sparkled and his mustache raised in a smile as he glanced over at Grace.

"Come on. You're not that much older than my baby sister." Ashley followed his gaze. He was clearly smitten by her sister.

"Just a mite. But I'm glad you think so."

Ashley turned back to her sister. "Why didn't you tell me?"

"And ruin the surprise? No way." Grace glowed with happiness, her brown hair pulled back from her forehead by a headband and falling in soft curls on her shoulders rather than caught up in her usual ponytail.

"No ponytail?"

"Not tonight. Tonight's a special occasion. One that comes once every ten years."

"Hopefully we won't have to wait that long for the next visit." Ava joined the group. "Your dad's late."

"Nothing new there," Grace said.

"But he's on his way. Let's sit outside while I get the grill started." Ava directed them out the back door to the patio. Ashley remembered many of her dad's cook-outs when she was growing up. Her dad loved to grill, and rest of the family loved to eat what he cooked. There was nothing special, just burgers, brats, ribs. Your traditional BBQ fare. Nothing she cared for. What made them special was the love that exuded from her father. Every weekend as long as there was good weather, her dad grilled. More everyday goodness.

"I picked up a black bean burger for you, Ashley. I hope that's okay," Ava said.

"Perfect." Ashley sat down next to her sister. "When are you due?"

"Not for another four months."

"Five months and already showing? Going to be a big baby, like the baby's daddy," Ashley joked. "You are, of course, going to name the baby after your favorite sister. Ashley, if it's a girl. Ashley, if it's a boy." Ashley pretended to be serious then laughed when Grace believed her. "Just kidding."

"We haven't picked out a name yet, but I'll keep it in mind."

Grace was always so considerate. Ashley knew she wouldn't name the baby after her. Why would she? She hadn't exactly been the best sister, hadn't even made it to Grace's wedding last November. Yet Grace didn't even mention it. Yes, Grace was by far the good one of the three kids. She deserved to be happy. Ashley looked over at Abel, who was helping Ava with the grill.

"He looks like a keeper," Ashley commented. "You know, I'm sorry. Missing your wedding and all. We were going into production of *Nutcracker*."

"We got your salad spinner," Grace said.

"Williams Sonoma. Best little salad spinner around."

Grace shrugged. "It's okay. It wasn't exactly unexpected. You haven't attended any family events over the past ten years."

Did Ashley catch a hint of recrimination in Grace's words? If so, it was barely a hint. How could Grace be so accepting? How did she deserve a sister like Grace?

"But don't be a stranger. I want our baby to know Aunt Ashley."

"Aunt Ashley. I like the sound of that." Leave it to Grace to be so … grace filled. Their parents knew what they were doing when they named her. Why hadn't they been closer? Oh, yeah. Because Ashley had blamed Grace for their mother's death. No small matter. Not that she ever said so to Grace. It was unspoken. Sometimes the unspoken is more powerful than the spoken.

"I'm sorry we haven't been closer. I'll make it up to you by being the best Aunt Ashley ever."

"Just be yourself and show up now and then. That's enough."

"That I can do. I promise." Ashley even meant it.

They sat down to a meal of her dad's burgers and her stepmom's barbecued spareribs—an orgy of meat. The smell both tantalized and repulsed her. Yes, this was her childhood dinner table where meat was always the centerpiece of every meal. And bacon! Bacon was served in crisp slices for breakfast, sprinkled on salads, added to casseroles and deviled eggs, and used as a condiment for burgers and sandwiches. Everything tasted better with bacon, or so she had been told. Was it any wonder she had rebelled as a teen, her being a vegetarian and all?

But then, there was her family, sitting around the same table. There were sweet memories of holiday dinners with extended family. Nothing like the quiet meals she ate alone in her apartment or on the go between rehearsals. Or the boisterous gatherings with other dancers where meat was relegated to a lesser role.

"No bacon?" Ashley commented as burgers were passed around.

"We do have pork spareribs. That's our bacon substitute." Her dad reached for a slab of ribs. "Don't you think bacon would have been overkill?"

"Never too much bacon." Abel grabbed a burger. "Or cheese."

"There's a man after my own heart," her dad said.

"We have cut back some on red meat, haven't we dear?" Ava added. "More chicken and fish. We even do meatless meals now and then."

"As long as there's piles of cheese," Grace said. "Not exactly a heart-healthy alternative."

Ashley smiled and looked down at her bean burger. She had removed the bun and added lettuce and a thick slice of tomato. A little cheese would be good, might make it palatable. But she wouldn't let on. She appreciated her stepmother had made the effort. Tomorrow she would go to the grocery store. Not every bean or veggie burger was equal. Some were definitely better than the others. Fortunately, there was potato salad, a mixed spring lettuce salad and watermelon.

"Oh, Ashley," Ava addressed her. "I pulled out some of the boxes of your stuff from the attic. Thought maybe you would like to go through it while you are here."

"And if you would like to take some of it home with you ..." her dad added.

"That's not the reason for doing this. I thought Ashley would enjoy looking at some of her old stuff, programs from recitals, videotapes, costumes."

"Though it would be nice to clean out the attic some."

"Ashley can keep her stuff in our attic as long as she wants, until she has a house of her own." Ava told her dad then turned to her. "I know there's no room for excess boxes in your apartment."

"But once you have a house of your own, Ava and dad will be happy to have it off their hands," Grace said. "As I well know."

"Thanks Ava." Ashley came to her stepmother's defense. "It might be nice to go through my stuff from high school."

"See," Ava told Dale. "I told you she would like it."

The conversation lulled as mouths were filled with the savory foods. Ashley broke the quiet. "Dad, why didn't you tell me Caleb was working for you?"

"Who?" Her dad put down the bone he had just stripped of meat and wiped his hands on a napkin.

"Caleb. Caleb Marshall. Remember him? My high school boyfriend."

"I didn't know you wanted to know."

Ashley turned to her stepmother. "And why didn't you let me know he had moved back to Cascade Falls?"

"I thought I did. He moved back after his mother died."

"No, I would have remembered that."

"Well, you didn't exactly seem interested in what was happening here. I'm sure I must have mentioned it. Why?"

Good question. Why did it matter to her? "Oh, nothing." Ashley shook her head and shrugged. "I ran into him at the dance studio."

"That's right. His little girl takes classes there," Ava said. "Sad about his mother and his wife. Did you know her? Stacy. Nice girl. She attended St. Luke's too. A grade or two behind you." A schoolteacher, Ava remembered all of her former students.

"How did he end up working for you, Dad? I don't remember him being interested in plumbing."

"He wasn't, but he needed a job, and I need good workers. Always do. Especially after Alex left to be Jacob's agent."

"Wait. Alex was working there too? And now he's Jacob's agent?"

"I'm sure I wrote you about it. Just like I wrote you about Caleb." Her stepmother reached for the salad and passed it around. "No bacon, just for you," Ava said as Ashley piled the greens on her plate next to a small scoop of potato salad. "What's the matter? You don't like my potato salad? You always liked it as a girl."

"I do like it, but mayonnaise ..." Ashley shook her head.

"It seems our dad has a soft spot for young men in need of a job," Grace said.

"Not a soft spot. It's just good business. If someone's reliable and a hard worker, I can train them. That's better than someone who is lazy and comes in late, or doesn't come in at all, no matter how much he may know about plumbing. Besides, Caleb took Alex's position as sales and marketing director. He's good at it too. Since no one in the family seems interested in the family business, I have to look elsewhere." At one point, her cousin Scot had been working for her dad. He had since moved on to a bigger company in a bigger city with more pay to support his growing family.

"Don't believe everything Dad says," Grace told her. "Dad has a reputation for being a good employer. He treats everybody fairly, with respect, and is understanding about family obligations. That was a draw for Caleb, him being a single parent."

They finished the meal with carrot cake from a local bakery.

"Why spend the time and effort baking when you have an excellent bakery nearby," Ava commented as she cut the cake.

Ashley allowed herself a sliver.

"Is that all?" Ava questioned.

"You have no idea how hard I will have to work tomorrow to pay for the calories I just ate."

"That's all right, Ava," Grace stretched out her plate for a piece. "You can give me Ashley's share. I am eating for two, you know."

"Yes, we know," her parents and Abel said in unison.

Ashley smiled as she nibbled the piece of cake on her plate. It tasted like home.

After Ashley went upstairs, she searched her carry-on luggage for her jewelry box, ignoring the boxes her stepmom had left stacked in the corner of the room. Time enough tomorrow to look at them. She opened her jewelry box and looked through the contents. She hadn't brought a lot, but what she brought was good. Elegant gifts from suitors to adorn her bare chest or dangle from her ears with her hair swept up in a chignon. She was prepared.

She pulled out the diamond engagement ring Michael had given her. She had taken it off before she left New York and put it into her jewelry box. It would have been a complete give away to her family. She wanted to choose the right time to tell everyone. She put it on her finger and admired how it sparkled even in this dim light. Michael had chosen well. He was everything she wanted in a beau, and more. She took the ring off and tucked it in a corner.

In the other corner she found a simple class ring, wrapped in tissue paper. It was Caleb's. Two sizes too big for her finger. He had given it to her before she left for New York. No strings attached. No commitment or promise of one to come. Just a gift to remember him. She had silently promised she would never forget him. Another promise broken by the years.

At first, she had carried it with her, wrapping string around it to fit her finger, or hanging it from her neck like a necklace. It was a promise and a reminder. When it felt like she had lost herself in this new life, new city, New York, she would touch that ring and be reminded where she came from, who she was. As she became more comfortable in her surroundings, she started leaving it behind, tucking the ring into a safe place in her sock drawer until she had jewelry that warranted a jewelry box. Then it was relegated to that corner where she had almost forgotten it. Almost, but not entirely.

She slipped the ring on her finger. No, she hadn't grown into it. How had she forgotten Caleb? Not possible. She examined the ring from every angle then slipped it off and placed it back into the corner. Maybe it was time to give it back.

Chapter 7

Ashley had been determined to get an earlier start to her day, but it was so luxurious to sleep late, until summoned downstairs by the overpowering aroma of coffee.

"Just toast and fruit for me," Ashley said before Ava could crack an egg into the frying pan.

"But you need protein to keep going. How about a poached egg or two? No butter, no cheese, no bacon. I promise."

"If you put it that way." Ashley accepted the mug of coffee from her stepmother and raised her eyebrows. "No cinnamon?"

"If you have it every day, it won't be special anymore."

"Every day home is special."

"Remember you said that when the novelty wears off," Ava warned her.

"Novelty? Would the novelty wear off? Doesn't seem possible." Ashley soaked up the everyday goodness. It was like she was a stranger visiting a new planet. A planet that felt oddly familiar. "When are Josie and Jacob getting here?"

"Jacob couldn't get away until Friday, but Josie will be here tomorrow."

"Good. It's about time I meet this vixen who captured the heart of the heartbreak kid."

"You know Josie. She was here all the time when Grace wasn't at her house with her."

"That was then, back when she was my annoying little sister's friend. I need to meet the new Josie, the adult Josie, my future sister-in-law." Ashley didn't want to admit to what she knew her stepmom already knew. She had hardly paid her brother or sister any attention, much less their friends. She had a lot to make up for. Besides, Jacob, the pro-basketball player was much more interesting than Jacob her pimple-faced younger brother. She remembered Josie as a quiet shadow to her pesky sister. Someone who was around all the time, but not worth noticing. Perhaps she had been wrong.

"So, what's on the agenda today?" Ava sat two poached eggs on toast in front of her.

"First practice."

"And then …?"

"Maybe food shopping, exploring, see how Cascade Falls has changed. Or not."

"Perfect. I'm in."

"Wait." Ashley didn't remember inviting her stepmother along on her trip down memory lane.

"You don't know where anything is anymore."

"That's the fun of exploring. And I have my navigation system."

"I'll show you all the places you need to see." Ava ignored her reticence.

Maybe the novelty was wearing off already. Ashley shrugged. It was only two weeks. What would it hurt to humor her stepmother?

Ashley glanced into Studio One after finishing her practice. The girls came running past her, oblivious to her presence. This was not going to be as easy as she thought. Clearly the mystique of being a prima ballerina didn't impress them the way it did the adoring throngs that attended her performances in New York. She would have to find a way to work her magic.

She looked for Olivia amid the squirming girls. Maybe she would run into Caleb again? Instead. a young, professional looking woman breezed past her and swept up the girl.

"Aunt Chelsea." Ashley heard Olivia say.

"Your dad couldn't get away, so you're stuck with me."

Chelsea? Ashley didn't remember Caleb having a sister, especially not a younger one. Was that yet another person she had failed to notice in high school?

"Can we get ice cream?" Ashley heard as they waited for the elevator.

Chelsea put Olivia down. "And what would your father say?"

"Yes!"

"Olivia …" The woman faked a frown.

"Only if I eat my lunch first." Olivia pouted.

"Right. So we won't tell him." The woman took Olivia by the hand as they both laughed, co-conspirators in the plot to fool Olivia's dad. Ashley felt a strange tug as she watched the two, wrapped in their own little world. Like she had been with Aunt Kathleen.

"Something bothering you?"

Ashley jumped as Aunt Kathleen interrupted her thoughts.

"No, nothing." Ashley looked from Olivia to the remaining girls in the Studio.

"Don't lie to me. I know that look." Aunt Kathleen followed her gaze. "It's not like New York, Ashley. If you want to make an impression on these girls, it will take more effort than to just show up."

Now how did her aunt know what she was thinking? "Why would I worry about making an impression on these girls? I'll be gone after two weeks. What do I care what they think of me?"

"Because you can't help but make an impression on others. All you have to do is show up. But it won't be as easy as that with these girls. Join me for lunch and we can talk about how to win them over."

"Sorry. I think Ava has my day planned, along with a trip down memory lane."

"I know that place. And I know your stepmom's need to plan everything out." Her aunt smiled. "How about tomorrow?"

"Sure. I'll pencil it in."

"Ink it in." Her aunt was not to be dissuaded. Ashley liked that. "Oh, and Chloe has arranged for some of her older students to come in tomorrow afternoon."

Before Ashley could say she would check her schedule, Aunt Kathleen stopped her. "Don't worry. It's all arranged. I already checked with Ava. You are free, or were free tomorrow. Now you are booked."

Ashley checked her phone once she got into her rental car. One voice mail from a number she didn't recognize. She listened. Her doctor's office.

She'd had her mammogram on Friday, fitting it in before she left. Because of her mom's history of breast cancer, she had a mammogram every year. It was routine. She had also been tested for BRAC1 and 2 genes to indicate the likelihood of getting cancer. So far so good. No indication that she would inherit this form of her family plague.

"Please call the office as soon as possible, Ms. Reese," was the message. Funny. Usually they left the results on her voice mail. Ashley waited till she got home and was sitting in the driveway before returning the call.

"Yes, the doctor wants to talk to you. When can you come in?"

"I'm out of town for my brother's wedding. Can it wait?"

"I'll see if the doctor is available."

Ashley was surprised to hear the voice of her doctor. He never made phone calls, always left that to the receptionist or assistants.

"Ashley, this is Dr. Lincoln."

"Hi, doctor. Why the phone call?"

"It seems we've noticed an abnormality on your mammogram, in your left breast."

"An abnormality?"

"Yes, a small lump and a dense mass. With your mother's history of breast cancer, I'd like to have it checked out as soon as possible."

"I'm in Michigan for my brother's wedding. I'll be back in two weeks. Can't it wait till then?"

"I'd rather not. How far are you from Ann Arbor?"

"Not far. Thirty to forty minutes."

"I know a specialist at University of Michigan hospital. One of the best. I'll see if I can get you in this week for a biopsy."

"This week?"

"Yes. That will work for you, won't it?"

"I guess it will have to."

"Good. I'll have my office call you with the information on the appointment."

That was that. No words of reassurance, just that she had a mass. Ashley sat in the car staring at her phone until jarred back into the present by a knock on her window. Her stepmother.

"Ashley, what are you doing? You've been sitting here for twenty minutes. Is something wrong?"

"No, nothing's wrong." Ashley shook her head.

"Let me in," Ava insisted. Ashley hit the button to unlock the car doors. Ava slipped into the passenger side seat. "Tell me what's wrong."

"Nothing—"

"Ashley ..." Her stepmother stared intently at her. "You're not fooling me. I know something's wrong. What is it?"

"Okay." Ashley took a deep breath. "I just talked to my doctor."

"And ..."

"There's a lump and a suspicious mass in my left breast. He wants it biopsied."

"Oh." Ava sat quietly. She was aware of Ashley's mom's history with breast cancer. "You did get checked for BRAC1 and 2 a while back, didn't you? I know Grace did."

Ashley nodded.

"That's good then, right? You don't have that so that decreases the chance that you have breast cancer."

"Decreases it but doesn't eliminate it. I just know. I think I've always known I was fated to get breast cancer, just like my mom." As Ashley spoke the words, they became real to her, threatening to swallow her in despair at the tragic ending she knew awaited.

"You don't know that. It's just a lump. Lots of women have lumps. They get them biopsied and … nothing."

"Not every woman's mother died from breast cancer. I should have known. I'm the same age as my mom when she was diagnosed."

"That doesn't mean anything."

"Maybe that's why I never married or had kids. I didn't want them to go through what I went through as a kid." The more she talked about it the more certain she was about her destiny.

"You sure it didn't have something to do with your career?" Ava suggested.

"No. I knew there was a reason why it wasn't happening." Ashley's brain kept going faster and faster, jumping to conclusions faster than the Russian dancers in *The Nutcracker*.

"Slow down, Ashley. Let's not jump to any conclusions. Let's wait for the biopsy and results before you jump into a grave and cover yourself with flowers. Besides, treatment options have improved tremendously since your mom had breast cancer. When is the biopsy?"

"I don't know yet. He's going to have his office schedule it with a doctor at U of M, then let me know."

"You let me know. I'll go with you. You don't have to go through this alone. Your dad will want to come too."

"No, don't tell Dad. He'll just worry. Don't tell anyone till we know for sure. I don't want to spoil Jacob's wedding."

Ava stared at her before agreeing. "Okay. But you'll have to let your dad know sooner or later."

"Not if it's nothing."

"Let's hope for that. In the meantime, try not to dwell on it. Let's go inside and let me pamper you. Lemonade? Finger cookies? Wine? Whatever you want."

"Maybe just a little." What's a few calories? After all, she had just been given a death sentence.

Chapter 8

Ashley sat on the deck sunning herself, while Ava ran to the store to pick up food on Ashley's acceptable list. Not that it mattered. However, a glass or two of wine and some chocolate chip cookies and she was feeling better. Ava was right. No sense in worrying until she knew more. And no sense in letting anyone else know. She had the monopoly on worry.

She remembered the small back porch from her childhood. It had been replaced by a deck with room for a table and chairs and two lounge chairs for sunbathing. She missed the old porch. She remembered how Lucky, their dog, had run under the porch that day she brought him home. And then, how he hid there before he died. How she and Grace had crawled under the porch with him. Now a patio extended under and beyond the deck, adding another layer of places for hosting family gatherings.

Ashley was surprised by the sound of voices coming through the kitchen.

"Look who I brought home." Her dad walked out on the deck followed by Caleb. "Seems he was all alone for dinner, so I invited him to join us."

"Dad!" Ashley jumped up. Here she was, swilling down wine with cookie crumbs on her caftan. She had neglected to change after coming home from practice.

"No need to thank me. I figured you two old friends would enjoy having some time for catching up. I'm going to help Ava put away groceries then change out of my work clothes."

Ashley heard her dad and stepmom talking in the kitchen, leaving her alone with Caleb. "I'm sorry, Caleb. I wasn't expecting company. I haven't even changed my workout clothes. I've just been sitting here on the deck enjoying the fresh air and sunshine."

"I wouldn't expect you to be doing anything else. You're on vacation. Mind if I join you?" Caleb pulled up a chair and sat down, not waiting for her response.

"Not at all. Where's Olivia?"

"She's spending the night with her aunt."

"I saw her at the dance studio. I didn't know you had a sister."

"That's because I don't. Chelsea's my wife's sister."

"That explains it."

"Explains what?" Ava came out with a beer for Caleb. "If you want to change, I'll keep Caleb company."

"Yes, I would like to change." Ava to the rescue. Ashley took a quick shower then put on a summer top over capris and slipped on sandals. She combed her wet hair and tossed it before heading back downstairs. She figured she would let her hair dry in the sun. Besides, some people consider wet hair a fashion statement.

When she came downstairs, she heard quiet conversation coming from the deck as her parents talked with Caleb. She tossed her hair again and breathed in deep to clear her head from the wine fog. Maybe this was just what she needed tonight.

She joined them, taking a swig out of Caleb's beer before sitting down, ignoring the surprised looks on the faces of those gathered.

Over dinner, Ashley found herself without words. The conversation went on without her. Local gossip and stories about her when she was a little girl. Rather than embarrass her, the stories made her smile, even when they didn't match her memories. She looked about the table and again marveled at the ordinary goodness present there, something she had been missing without even knowing she did.

"Why so quiet, Ash?" her dad asked. "Aren't you going to give us your side of the story and tell Caleb how we got it all wrong?"

"No, Dad. It's perfect just the way you tell it." She smiled at the surprised look on her father's face.

"What happened to my little girl while you were in New York?"

"Though he did get it wrong," she told Caleb. "It was nothing like my dad said."

"That's the Ashley I remember." Her dad smiled at Caleb and winked at her. "Remember Ashley's excursion into the world of Irish step dancing? All that makeup and big hair," her dad teased.

"I never went in for that. I didn't like the costumes and fake hair. That's why I had Ava do my hair for me." Ashley was lured further into the conversation.

"That's right. I spent hours curling your hair so you wouldn't need a wig," Ava said.

"It wasn't that bad. And I did like the dancing, just not what went with it."

"You were good at it. A natural," her dad added. "Like everything related to dance. You are your mother's daughter."

Ashley and Ava exchanged glances.

"It's good you were able to come over tonight," Ava said to Caleb. "It seems Ashley is in high demand." She turned to Ashley. "Your grandmother and aunt are both requesting more of your time. They want you to have dinner with them tomorrow. And then Thursday I think you'll be getting fitted for your dress, along with the other bridesmaids and Josie. And then there's the bachelorette weekend."

"Bachelorette weekend?" her dad asked. "Since when has that been a thing?"

"Since weddings have become bigger and bigger productions. It isn't enough to have a party. Some brides have a girls' weekend away with their bridesmaids. I've heard of brides and their bridesmaids going to Jamaica or Las Vegas for the weekend. Josie isn't doing that, but she does have something planned for Friday night through Saturday night. Then Sunday there's the bridal shower."

"You do have a busy schedule. It's good you are able to fit in some time with us," her dad said. "And what are we men to do while this is going on?"

"Jacob will be having a bachelor party. You're both invited," Ava said.

"You're in the wedding?" Ashley asked Caleb.

"I'm not a groomsman, but I have been asked to usher. You forget, Jacob and I played basketball together in high school. And I worked with Alex with the high school team before Alex got 'called up' to the big league by your brother. We are a band of brothers, united by basketball."

"I guess I'm not the only one with a busy schedule," Ashley said.

"Things will calm down during the week before the wedding weekend," Ava said.

"Wedding weekend?" Dad asked.

"Yes. Friday there's the rehearsal and rehearsal dinner." Ava started listing off the activities. "Saturday, the wedding and reception. Then Sunday morning, brunch when the bride and groom open presents before heading out for their honeymoon."

"I'm glad we didn't have to go through all of that. This is getting too complicated for me. It's good Josie has you and her mom to keep everything straight. You just tell me where I have to be, and I'll show up." Her dad stood and picked up his plate. "What's for dessert?"

"I'm sorry, dear. You didn't let me know we were having a guest over, so I didn't plan anything."

"We don't have to have a guest to have dessert."

"Ashley and Caleb can always get ice cream from Frosty King if they want. It's a nice night for a walk," Ava suggested.

"Frosty King? Are they still open?" Ashley's mouth salivated at the suggestion. "I don't know that that's on my accepted food list." What would a small hot fudge sundae hurt? Or a large one?

Ashley rose and started to clear her plate. Caleb stood as well.

"You two let us take care of the dishes. There's still plenty of daylight left. Go and enjoy it. Sit on the deck while we clean up," Ava told them.

"How'd I end up volunteered for kitchen duty?" her dad asked.

"Let these two young people have some time together. Then I'll walk with you to Frosty King."

"Sounds like a plan."

Ava smiled at Ashley as she led her dad out.

Ashley looked at Caleb and shrugged. Who was she to insist on helping in the kitchen when there was a perfectly good deck to sit on?

The conversation lulled as Ashley and Caleb sat on the deck and Caleb finished off his beer.

"Pretty obvious set-up, though I did want to see you." Caleb sat his beer bottle down. "You want to get out of here?"

Ashley readily agreed, yelling into the kitchen to let her dad and Ava know they were leaving.

"Where are you taking me?" Ashley climbed into the passenger seat of Caleb's truck.

"Where would you like to go?"

"Everywhere."

"That can be arranged. But first places first."

"And that will be?"

"You'll see."

They rode in silence until Caleb pulled into the park. The thought of Michael tugged at her conscience, telling her this wasn't a good idea. But Ashley didn't want to think about Michael or anything else – especially the possibility of having breast cancer. She wanted to forget about everything that had to do with her life in New York, if only for tonight.

Ashley jumped out and ran to the tree where they had met. "I was hoping you would take me here."

"You were? Why didn't you say something? Why leave it to chance?"

"Because, if chance would have it be so, then it was meant to be." She touched the tree, allowing her fingers to caress the rough bark, as if doing so would transport her back to a time when she was young, had no responsibilities except to be a kid. Had there ever been a time like that? When had the obsession to make it into The Company taken root and taken over her life? She had missed out on so many of the fun events of high school, the prom, homecoming. All because she had been determined to be a ballet dancer in New York. Was it worth it? Worth all she had given up?

"You aren't making any more sense now than when we were kids." Caleb stood back, allowing her the moment as she leaned against the tree. She caught the slight smile on his face. Did he feel it too? Were they kids again?

"I wanted you to know instinctively this was where I wanted to go. Then it would be Kismet." Caleb shook his head. He was just as clueless now as when they had been kids. She didn't mind.

"Kismet?"

"Fate." How could he not know about kismet/fate? Oh, right. This was Caleb. He was never one for flights of fancy.

"You believe in fate?" Caleb asked.

"Something wrong with that?"

"Some people believe in God."

"Oh, him." Ashley shrugged.

"You still don't believe?"

"You still do? I thought you would have outgrown that by now."

Caleb didn't respond. There was a look on his face she didn't understand. He gazed beyond her across the expanse of the park, then tilted his head and raised his shoulders slightly.

"Tell me about yourself, Ashley Reese, prima ballerina. Never married? Boy friends?"

Now would be the time to tell him about Michael, but why spoil a fun night with mention of a fiancé who was miles away? To mention Michael would bring up her life in New York and all that meant. "You might say I'm married to my job. Though not for lack of opportunity." She moved to the other side of the tree where Caleb couldn't see her face and catch her in the lie.

"I figured as much."

Ashley pushed out her lower lip in a slight pout. "Although …" Why couldn't she tell him about Michael? This was Caleb. She could talk to him.

"There's someone?"

"He's coming to the wedding. You'll meet him then." That was enough information. She came back from where she had been partially hidden behind the tree. "And you?"

"You know I was married."

"Yes, to Stacey." Ashley grabbed hold of a branch of the tree and climbed up to where she could look out across the park. How many years had it been since she had last climbed this tree? She sat down on the branch and motioned for Caleb to join her.

"You sure it will hold us?"

"Are you scared?" she teased.

Caleb paused as if trying to come up with an excuse for refusing the challenge, then smiled and started up the tree.

"Tell me about Stacy," Ashley said once he was sitting next to her. "How did you meet?"

"I came back here after my mom died. I met her through St. Luke's. What can I say? It was a hard time. Even at the best, my relationship with my dad was strained. Without my mom as a buffer …" His voice trailed off.

When he didn't continue, she asked, "Then why did you come back?"

"I'm not sure. I guess it seemed like the right thing to do. Dad did need me. And then I met Stacy." The sun was making its progress across the sky to its resting place below the horizon. Caleb stared across the expanse of the park. "I knew her in passing in high school, but never paid much attention. I was preoccupied elsewhere." He turned and smiled at Ashley.

"As well you should have been." She turned away from his gaze and fixed her eyes on the horizon.

"Stacy helped me get through the loss of my mom. She had a way of smiling that made you just know everything would be okay. She even had a way with my dad. She filled the hole in my life, in my heart. What can I say? With Stacy, everything was easy, like we fit."

"Unlike me." Ashley wasn't upset at the thought. She knew what she had been like back then. Besides, this was Caleb. She could talk to him.

"You were pretty high maintenance. And independent. It was like I could hardly get you to admit we were more than friends."

"I was afraid you would keep me from doing what I was determined to do."

"Like anyone could. I never wanted to hold you back. And now, look at you." He turned sideways to make his point, turning away from the setting sun and smiling directly at her. "A prima ballerina. Everything you dreamed of. You did it. I'm proud of you."

"And look at you, a dad, living in Cascade Falls. Something I never expected," Ashley teased, lightly punching his arm.

"Cascade Falls isn't so bad. I realized that after I left. And being a dad … best thing ever. Olivia helped me keep going after Stacy's death. I had to keep going to take care of her." He stared back across the park at the fading colors of the sunset.

The evening had taken a somber turn that Ashley had been trying to avoid. She didn't want to think about death or motherless girls. Not tonight. It would be all too easy to sink into a pity party if she let herself go there. As if he read her mind, Caleb changed the subject.

"Have you kept up with your guitar?"

Ashley laughed. "Heck no. Guitars would never fit in the life of a ballerina."

"Too bad. It was fun."

"What about you?"

"Me? Why I'm part of the most famous garage band on Thirty Second Street."

"No way." Ashley laughed. This was the Caleb she remembered.

"Way." Caleb laughed back at her. "You'll have to hear us sometime. Maybe even stand in on a set. Maybe tonight." Caleb jumped down from the tree then waited for her, catching her when she landed.

"Oh, I don't know."

"Sure. Come on. It'll be fun." Caleb raced for the car, leaving her to catch up.

"Where are we going?" She was out of breath yet laughing when she reached his car.

"To my garage. I've got an extra guitar. I'll call the other band members. Olivia is gone for the night. Let's do some head-banging!"

Chapter 9

Wow! Her head throbbed. That was some head banging last night. Ashley's mouth hung open and was coated from the previous night's escapade. There had been more than head banging. She had thrown back a few too many beers. Oh, the calories! She would pay for this. The aroma of coffee that had been so enticing the other morning triggered her gag reflex. Did she need to run to the bathroom?

But it was fun. Who'd have thought that not only were the other members of her old band still around, but they also were married with kids. Jesse, their bass player, and Kara, their drummer, had married right out of high school. Filling in for her was Geri, another high school friend, or so Caleb informed her. Ashley didn't remember her, but if Caleb said she was a friend, she believed him.

She hadn't wanted to play at first. It had been a long time since she had held a guitar in her hands. She could only remember a few basic chords. But, after a few beers, she made those chords echo throughout the garage, banging on the guitar and singing like a banshee. It was a release, like screaming with a beat. After the discipline of ballet, she needed a release. Her fingertips were bloody from holding down the metal strings.

"You have to build up your calluses again," Caleb told her when she complained.

"That's for you, not me. The only calluses I have are on my feet, especially my toes." She kicked off her sandals to show the rough cracked corns on her toes. "Some nights I sit with a bag of frozen peas on my feet and cry." Now why had she told them that?

"Doesn't sound all that glamorous to me." Geri cracked open two beers and handed one to Caleb in a familiar manner that caused the hairs on the back of Ashley's neck to stand up. Geri sat on the arm of the overstuffed chair where Caleb sat. Ashley turned away and talked to Jesse and Kara.

"Who's watching your kids?"

"The oldest, Jessica, is fourteen. She watches the younger ones. Besides, Kara's mom lives with us."

"Though some days she needs watching almost as much as the kids," Kara said. "Early-stage Alzheimer's."

"I'm sorry."

"Don't be. We love having her around and on her better days she helps with the kids."

"Your oldest is fourteen?" Ashley did the math in her head. "You must have started early. I've been gone for fifteen years."

"Yes, senior year, after you left. It was the scandal of the high school. Kara was pregnant at graduation. We graduated, married, and along came Jessica. Maybe not the best start for a marriage, but it seems to be working for us," Jesse said.

"I didn't even realize you were dating."

"Neither did most people. We were band members first. It just developed, like you and Caleb."

"You were a 'thing' in high school?" Geri asked.

"You wouldn't have known it." Kara tipped her beer and nodded at Ashley. "Caleb was all about basketball and work back then. Ashley was all about dancing, but, yeah, they were."

Geri eyed Ashley in a way that made her squirm, or was that the alcohol? With that exchange, Ashley's unsettled stomach rebelled. She ran for the door and managed to get outside before throwing up in some bushes alongside the garage. Jesse and Kara drove her home, since Caleb had had too much to drink too.

"If it's any consolation, your dad said Caleb looked worse than you when he came into work today." Her stepmother came in with a tray with dried toast and tea.

"Coffee smells awful."

"That's why I brought tea—chamomile. I thought it would be easier on your stomach." Ava sat down on the end of her bed. "What happened last night?"

"Nothing. We went to the park, then we went to Caleb's garage and played music. Jesse and Kara came over. Just like in high school. Only in high school there was never any beer."

"Better not have been." Ava frowned before adding, "Your aunt Kathleen called. Said to remind you about lunch today."

"Lunch. That's right." Ashley sat up in bed. "What time is it?" Ashley reached for her phone and noticed four missed calls. One last night from Michael. How could she have forgotten to call him? Two from Aunt Kathleen plus a text message. And one more from New York—must be her doctor's office.

"It's eleven o'clock. Kathleen is expecting you at noon. She called me. Said she couldn't get through to you."

"I've got to shower."

"That you do. And try to get something into your stomach."

Ashley grimaced but picked up the toast and took a bite. She put it back down when Ava left and then checked her messages.

Michael. "Ashley, dear, checking on you to make sure you're still alive. You did make it safely to … wherever it was you went, Cascade something? Anyway. I wanted to give you some time with your family before calling. Time's up. Call me when you can. When you are free from all of your wedding responsibilities." He didn't sound angry. His voice had a teasing tone, but he made his point.

Ashley texted him. "Sorry. Went to a friend's home last night. Will call later." No sense in calling now. She knew Michael would be at work.

Then she listened to Kathleen's messages. "Ashley, wake up! I'm calling to confirm lunch today at noon. Call me back."

Then the call from her doctor's office. "We have a nine o'clock appointment for you Monday morning with Dr. Clark at U of M. You need to come an hour early for prep. Make sure you have someone to drive you as you won't be able to drive afterwards.

We'll be sending an email with further instructions. Call us if you have any questions." She checked her email. There it was waiting for her to open. This was going to happen. But not yet. Not today. Today she needed to shower. Plenty of time to read through the instructions when she got back.

Ashley put down her phone and stumbled to the bathroom.

Chapter 10

Lunch with Aunt Kathleen. How long had it been since she had done this? So long she couldn't remember. She had stopped her weekly dinners and overnights about the time Aunt Kathleen had married Uncle Joe. Something about having a minister for an uncle put a damper on a party.

"You don't look so good," Aunt Kathleen said when she sat down. "What did you do last night?"

"A few too many beers with Caleb." Ashley ordered a veggie smoothie.

"Caleb? Isn't that the young man from that band you were in? You dated, didn't you?" Aunt Kathleen asked and placed her order, her usual hamburger, but this time no bacon or cheese and salad in place of French fries. And only water to drink. Some things do change.

"No bacon and cheese, or French fries?"

"Sometimes a gal's got to watch what she eats." Her aunt dismissed the question. "We were talking about Caleb, weren't we?"

"Yes." Why was everyone so unsure about their relationship? "Our relationship wasn't exactly a secret."

"No, we knew you were dating. But sometimes it seemed more like a convenience, someone to go out with but nothing serious."

Ashley shook her head. Was she really that bad? She wouldn't use Caleb just to say she had a boyfriend. Would she? What could she say to that? "Are you saying I used Caleb?"

"No, not at all. That's not what I meant. You were so focused on dance back then. Still are, I presume, based on how rarely you come home." Aunt Kathleen took a bite of her burger. "It's okay. It's just you. I always admired your spunk."

"I'm so sorry." Ashley didn't know what else to say. "I guess I didn't realize anyone missed me that much. I know I'm not always the most pleasant person to have around."

"You are who you are, who you had to be to achieve what you had set your heart on." Ashley didn't know what was worse. The matter-of-fact way that Aunt Kathleen said those things about her, or if she had tried to guilt her.

"And that wasn't Caleb." Ashley was surprised to admit it, though she recognized it was true. She sighed and took another sip of her smoothie. It was not going down.

"We all recognized that, including Caleb." Aunt Kathleen shrugged and finished off her burger.

Ashley knew it. Her family knew it. Even Caleb knew it. So why did it bother her? Yes, she had been focused, but what about family, friends? Enough of this.

"How are Josh and Scott doing?" Ashley changed the subject. Josh and Scott were her cousins, Aunt Kathleen's sons.

"Good. Or at least Scott is. He has three kids. You'll meet them at the wedding. His youngest, Brad, is going to be ring bearer."

"Who's the flower girl?"

"Didn't Caleb tell you? His daughter, Olivia."

"I didn't realize they were that close."

"Alex has a little girl, but she's only two. They weren't sure she would be able to do it so they got Olivia as a backup of sorts. If Shanda doesn't cooperate, they will still have a flower girl. If she does cooperate, they'll have two flower girls."

"Sounds like quite the production."

"Ava had something to say about it."

"As I'm sure she would." Ashley smiled. "What about Josh? Is he married?"

"No one has been able to get him to the altar, though not for lack of trying." Aunt Kathleen picked at her salad.

"And Joe's girls?"

"Michelle is married with two kids. Stephanie has the one son, Gus. You remember him, don't you?"

"Barely. He was just a baby when I left. That makes him, what? Fifteen?"

"All that." A proud smile crossed her aunt's face.

"Is Stephanie married?"

"She's been engaged a couple of times. For some reason they never worked out. I don't know what she's holding out for. She has a good job in sales and marketing."

"Still living in Cascade Falls?"

"Yes, but she's been offered a promotion, a bigger store in Chicago."

"Good for her. She's going to take it, isn't she? Who wouldn't want to live in Chicago?"

"Some say Cascade Falls isn't so bad. I lived in Chicago. It wasn't everything you young people think it is." Aunt Kathleen shook her head, silently admonishing Ashley.

"Not when you spend part of the time in the Cook County jail." Her aunt's checkered past was no secret to Ashley or any of the family.

Her aunt smiled back at her, choosing to not acknowledge what Ashley had said. Aunt Kathleen's past, however checkered, was still her past and put behind her. "Besides, she has Gus to think about. He hasn't graduated yet."

"What does Gus think about moving to Chicago?"

"He thinks it would be great, but what does he know? Enough of this."

Ashley ignored her aunt's last comment. "If Stephanie moves away, what will you and Uncle Joe do? There'll be none of your kids left in Cascade Falls."

"Actually, there was something I wanted to talk to you about." Her aunt paused for effect.

"You mean this isn't just a social lunch?"

"Not entirely, though you know how much I love seeing you." Aunt Kathleen took a sip of water and smiled at her.

"Okay. Spill it. What are you up to?"

"It's just, Joe's reaching retirement age, so am I. He's planning on retiring from St. Luke's soon. We already have an associate pastor ready to step into the position. Maybe you remember her, Gwen Thompson, though now she's Gwen Kelley. She was one of our interns."

"That was after I left."

"Anyway. It's all set for Joe."

"That's great. What about you? Is Chloe going to take over?"

Aunt Kathleen paused, took another drink of water, and looked over at her before continuing. "That's just it. Chloe has done a great job with the dance studio. She's also been a tremendous help to me over these years. But running the dance studio and running the Center for Arts and Healing, they're both full time. One person can't do both."

"So find yourself someone with business management skills to take over."

"It's not that simple. It can't be just anyone. We need someone with a love of the arts." Another pause as Aunt Kathleen looked sideways at her. "Someone like you."

"Whoa, someone like me? I don't have any business skills."

"Neither did I when I started. You can learn. Besides, I'm sure you know something about the business end of running a ballet company from your experience in New York. Meeting with patrons, giving them what they want, fundraising. Someone with your stature would draw more people to the dance studio. You could even put on world-class performances using your contacts from New York." Now there was no slowing her aunt down as she spun her web around Ashley.

"In Cascade Falls? Who would come? Aunt Kathleen, you're dreaming. It's crazy."

"Dream with me. Be a little crazy. Where's that determined girl I knew who wouldn't let anything get in her way? It's a challenge. And it would give you a chance to win over a whole new generation of girls to the arts." Aunt Kathleen stopped as she prepared her final snare. "If you won't consider it for me, consider it for your mother. It's her legacy." Trap set and baited.

"That's not fair." Ashley pulled loose from the web her aunt tried to entangle her in, anger swelling in her chest.

"At least say you'll think about it."

"No, I won't. I'm not giving up what I've worked all my life to achieve, not for you, not for the Center. And if my mother were here, she wouldn't have asked it of me. You know that."

"But do you? Do you really know what she would ask?"

"She would want me to be happy," Ashley asserted.

"That she would. Are you happy?"

"Of course, I am. I have it all. I dance the best roles in all the ballets performed by the premiere ballet company in America. I have a good life, and a boyfriend."

"A boyfriend. That's the first you've mentioned him."

"Well, I do. He's coming to the wedding. Why would I want to give all of that up to live in Cascade Falls?" Ashley glared at her aunt, daring her to respond.

"You can't blame a gal for trying." Her aunt shrugged her shoulders and took another sip of water.

"Yes, I can."

"Fair enough." Aunt Kathleen nodded in agreement. "It's not going to be awkward between us, is it? I would hate that."

"No." Ashley shook her head. The anger that had arisen so quickly just as quickly slipped away. "I would hate that too. You were there for me when my mom died. What would I do without you?"

"I had to give it a shot. You understand that, don't you? I miss you, Ashley. Would love to see you more."

"I do understand, and maybe I can do better about coming home." Ashley found herself smiling despite her previous anger. How could she stay angry at Aunt Kathleen? "What are you going to do?"

"I don't know, but I'll figure it out."

"You always do."

"Yes, but it's different now." Aunt Kathleen picked at what remained of her salad, then pushed the plate away, leaving the salad unfinished.

"How? If anything, the Center is flourishing. It shouldn't be hard to find someone who would take it on."

"It's not as simple as that. Nonprofits, they always live one year to the next, dependent on donors."

"Not all nonprofits." Ashley knew this from her experience with dance companies. Many were nonprofit as well. Some struggled but others were successful. Some were able to build up an endowment to keep them operating. If anything, it looked to her like her mom's legacy was solid.

"Well, then, this non-profit does."

"But you get rent from all of those businesses."

"That helps, but some of those businesses are struggling, hanging on by their fingernails. We give breaks to those. The money we make in rent isn't enough to cover all the expenses of keeping the building operational. We make ends meet but we haven't been able to save much over the years. All it takes is for us to lose a few renters and we'll be back in the red."

"The dance studio is profitable, isn't it?"

"Yes, for now. An economic downturn and parents won't be able to afford dance lessons for their kids."

"I know." Ashley had to give her aunt that. The arts were too often considered a non-essential when it came to funding. "That's just the reality of the arts."

"But that's okay. We'll manage."

"Maybe I can help."

"Like what?"

"Like maybe bring in some dancers to do a performance to raise money for the Center."

"That would be great. And I would love to have you come back to Cascade Falls. But even if you could pull it off, we need time to promote it and sell tickets. No, you're here for Jacob's wedding. That will take all your time. Forget I said anything."

Ashley knew Aunt Kathleen said to forget it, but she also recognized that Aunt Kathleen knew she wouldn't forget it. That's why Aunt Kathleen brought it up. How could she just forget about the dance studio her mother had started?

Chapter 11

Behind schedule, Ashley admonished herself as she rode the elevator with Aunt Kathleen to the dance studio after lunch. How could she have allowed herself to stay out so late and drink so much?

"Remember, you're coming over for dinner tonight. Grandma and Peter will be there," Aunt Kathleen said before they went separate ways — Kathleen to her office, her to Studio Two. Ashley glanced into Studio One. No squirming dancers in pink leotards. They were already gone for the day. That meant she missed Caleb, or Aunt Chelsea, or whomever was picking Olivia up today. No chance to work her magic on the girls. Just as well.

Her body was definitely rebelling. She had toxins to flush out. She couldn't take the day off. It was going to be hard enough to keep in shape with all the wedding activities ahead. She couldn't start letting herself go already. However, she did need the escape of last night. For just a few hours she had no longer been Ashley Reese, prima ballerina, or Ashley Reese, daughter of a cancer victim, or Ashley Reese, potential cancer victim. It was as if she had gone back in time to her teens. She had been Ashley Reese, teenager, member of a band, a friend. She liked that. It was a nice and necessary change. Maybe she could do it again before she left, without the alcohol to numb her mind and loosen her inhibitions.

It took some doing, but eventually she had her body back into some semblance of shape. One night wouldn't do her in. But two weeks of such nights … Not going to happen. She would make sure of that.

Chloe interrupted her concentration. "Ashley, the girls are here. Are you ready?"

"Ready? For what?"

"My advanced class. Your aunt did tell you about it, didn't she?"

"Oh, yes, sure." She had agreed to talk to Chloe's advanced class, hadn't she? Ready as she could be with a hangover.

A group of seven teenage girls slipped in, wearing leotards and toe shoes, giggling and chatting as they caught up with each other. Ashley recognized two of the girls as assistants from the morning dance camp. Patrice and Danielle.

"I thought maybe you could give them some tips. Help them with their stances," Chloe stated.

"Okay." Ashley hadn't known she would be teaching a class. That was so much better than just talking to the girls.

"Attention," Chloe called. The girls stopped their chatter and lined up along the barre. Chloe nodded to Ashley, her cue to take over.

Ashley put them through their paces, having them demonstrate each position, stretch on the barre, go up and down, plie, relevé. She walked among them, making adjustments, just like her ballet instructors had done for her so many times over the years. The tiredness fell away.

"Well done. You have a good teacher." Ashley nodded in the direction of Chloe. "Now do you have any routines to show me?"

"Do the dance from your recital. The piece from *Swan Lake*," Chloe told the girls then turned to Ashley. "I try to have the advanced class do something classical each year along with a more modern piece."

"I know. I remember."

Ashley couldn't help but smile as she watched. Far from perfect, the girls wavered on their toes and slipped. Their arms drooped at times, rather than holding up in a perfect arc. They weren't destined for New York, but they would love dance. Her mother's legacy would go on in these girls.

Afterwards, the girls came up to her and thanked her for her time.

"Could we do it again? Do you have time?" each asked in their own way.

"How about next Wednesday?" Chloe interjected.

Ashley was touched by their response. How could she say no? "Of course, I'll make sure my schedule is clear."

Ashley went straight to her room when she got home, opened the top box in the corner and searched. She wasn't sure what she was looking for until she found it. Her first pair of pointe shoes. She remembered how excited she had been when she finally got them. Since then, there had been too many pointe shoes to count. Pointe shoes did not arrive ready to wear. They needed to be molded and formed and ribbons attached. Each ballerina has her own ritual for getting a new pair ready to wear. So many hours put into banging shoes into shape. Professional ballerinas could go through a hundred to a hundred and twenty pairs a season. But there was always something special about that first pair.

She took down a picture from the wall and hung the shoes on the nail where it would remind her of how she had started, her youthful enthusiasm for dance. It wasn't gone, just needed to be reactivated.

She gazed at the shoes before opening the email with instructions for Monday. After reading it, she sighed, took one last look at her pointe shoes then went downstairs where she found Ava in the kitchen emptying the dishwasher.

"Ava, the biopsy is scheduled for Monday at nine. We have to be there by eight for prep. I'll send you the email."

"That will work." Ava continued putting away dishes.

"But we'll need to leave here a little after seven. What will we tell my dad?" How could she be so calm when Ashley's whole world was falling apart?

"That we are having a 'girl's' morning, starting with breakfast then shopping in Ann Arbor, just the two of us, before all the festivities begin." Ava put the last dish away and pointed to a chair at the table.

Ashley sat. "Will he believe that?"

"What do you think?"

"He'll be suspicious. I've never been one for early morning shopping trips."

Ava sat down next to her. "Then maybe you should tell him. You're going to have to tell him eventually. I can cover for you, but only so much. He'll know I'm keeping something from him — he already suspects. But he loves you too much to push you to tell him. He's waiting for you to come to him."

"I'm sorry, Ava." Ashley realized the truth in what Ava was saying. It wasn't like Ava, but it was like her. "I'm sorry I put you in the position of keeping something from my dad. Dad has always been so good to me. So patient."

"You didn't think so when he set curfews."

"That was then. He was looking out for me, like a parent should."

"He's still looking out for you."

"You're both so good to me and I'm the worst daughter ever." It felt good to beat up on herself.

"Not the worst." Ava smiled at her. "You were just being yourself—an ordinary teenager."

Ashley shuddered at the thought. "No, don't say that. I was never an ordinary anything."

"What's so bad about being ordinary?"

"Everything." How could she say that? How little her stepmom knew her.

"You're right. You always were the worst or the best. You never chose middle ground. Sounds like an ordinary teenager to me. And I know. I've dealt with enough of them. Maybe it's time to grow up, accept that it's okay to be ordinary."

Ashley frowned and shook her head. "Maybe for you. Ordinary fits you. But not me."

"Thanks, I think. You always enjoyed a good drama."

"What does that mean?" What was Ava talking about?

"Nothing, just that you are our Ashley and we love you. No matter what you do. Nothing will change that." Ava smiled again. It didn't feel reassuring. Why was she being so nice? "So, are you going to tell your dad? Or should I?"

"But if I tell him, he'll be upset."

"As is his right as a parent."

"Can't we wait a little longer?"

"It's up to you." Ava sighed. Ashley had won this one, as she knew she would.

"You're the best, Ava." Ashley kissed her then headed upstairs to get ready for dinner.

Chapter 12

Dinner at Aunt Kathleen's was uneventful, as expected. That was good.

"Aren't you coming?" she asked her dad and Ava before she left.

"No, your aunt Kathleen wanted you all to herself. She barely agreed to allow your grandmother to come and bring Peter. And, of course, your uncle Joe lives there, so she had to allow him."

Ashley didn't mind, as long as Aunt Kathleen didn't blind-side her again, trying to get her to move back to Cascade Falls.

But as it turned out, her aunt was on her best behavior, helping Uncle Joe serve the meal he cooked.

"I thought after all these years of marriage you would be a great cook," Ashley said.

"I'm a great cook. Watch how I do it." Her aunt picked up her phone and dialed for take-out. "See? Easy?" She laughed. "But I am better — aren't I, Joe?"

"I couldn't keep this slim figure without your aunt's cooking," he joked.

"Ha ha." Aunt Kathleen frowned. "I think I've been insulted. You keep laughing and you'll end up the only cook in this family once you retire."

"Isn't that how it already is?" Uncle Joe asked.

Aunt Kathleen leaned over and kissed him. "And how it better stay."

"Speaking of retirement. How is that going? Do you have a retirement date yet?" Peter asked.

"It's going well, on my part. Gwen is ready to step in whenever I'm ready to step down. The only hitch is finding someone to run the Center so Kathleen can retire and join me."

"Who says you both have to retire at the same time? Peter retired before me. That worked fine," Grandma Esther said.

"That was because you were too stubborn to turn over the reins of the Center to Kathleen," Peter said.

"No, I just wasn't ready. Kathleen will retire when she's ready," her grandma asserted.

"What are you going to do when you retire, Joe?" Peter asked.

"Travel. I'd like to see America while I can. And spend more time with the grandkids, especially the ones no longer living here."

"What about you, Kathleen?"

"Travel would be nice. But, like Mom said, I'll retire when I'm ready."

"Do you think your dad will be retiring soon?" Peter asked Ashley.

Her dad? Retire? Was he really that old?

Her grandmother spoke up before she could respond. "And give up that business of his? I doubt it. He wouldn't know what to do with himself if he didn't go to work every day. Ava, though, she's not far from retirement. It's hard work, being a teacher—emotionally draining."

"I guess I better be prepared to search for another sixth-grade teacher." Uncle Joe sighed.

"Leave that to the principal and the next pastor," her grandma said. "Enough of this old-people talk about retirement. Ashley, tell us about New York and the ballet."

Ashley was glad to have a change of topic. Grandma was right. Enough about retirement and people getting old. She hated to admit her parents, grandparents, aunt, and uncle, were all so much older than when she left.

She told them about *Giselle* and the *Sleeping Beauty* production coming up.

"But what I'm especially excited about is a new ballet, choreographed by one of the major new choreographers in New York. It will be a challenge to learn something new." Much as she loved the classics, it was nice to try something different. Still, she had to give the audience what they wanted, which meant … *Nutcracker* every December. *Swan Lake, Giselle, Sleeping Beauty* … sigh.

"That's lovely, dear," her grandmother said. "You wouldn't be interested in moving back to Cascade Falls and running the Center, would you?"

"Grandma!" Ashley's mouth dropped open. She frowned at Aunt Kathleen.

"I didn't put her up to this." Aunt Kathleen held up her hands in denial.

"What? Did I say something wrong?" Grandma asked.

Ashley relaxed, shook her head, and laughed. "No, Grandma. You never say anything wrong. For you, I'd maybe consider it. But you heard Aunt Kathleen, she's not ready to retire."

"That's settled then. Who's ready for pie?" Peter asked.

Chapter 13

It was an early night. Ashley appreciated that. That gave her time to call Michael before going to bed.

"I was beginning to wonder if you had forgotten me entirely. I was getting ready to book a flight and make sure you were still alive." Michael's tone was playful but she knew underneath the words was an ounce of seriousness.

"I'm sorry, Michael. It's been pretty busy."

"I'm sure there are lots of people who want your time. Just so you save some time for me."

Ashley squirmed. He had a point there. "Always, though it looks like this weekend I'll be spending with the other bridesmaids. First at a bachelorette weekend, then a bridal shower. So, if you don't hear from me …"

"Is this a Cascade Falls thing? All of this the weekend before the wedding, turning it into a two-week party?"

"No, not really. But since Jacob and Josie live in California it was too difficult to get everyone together at different times during the year. That's why Josie scheduled it like this."

"Why aren't they holding the wedding in California? San Francisco this time of year is beautiful." Michael had changed the subject, not her. Maybe he figured he had made his point.

"Because both their families live here. If I know Jacob, he probably wants a big blow-out wedding. He likes to do things in a big way."

"Not unlike his sister." Again Michael teased, though there was a softness this time. She could hear his smile even if she couldn't see him.

"No, I'm not like Jacob at all. I only want big blow-out events when it supports the arts."

"Precisely. When do I get to meet this famous basketball player?"

Ashley smiled despite her concern. Michael had a way of making her smile. "I didn't think you were interested in basketball."

"I'm interested in anything that involves you, but I do have other interests. Have you told your parents about me yet?"

Ooops. How could she tell him she still hadn't told them? "It hasn't come up. Sorry."

"How could it not come up?" Did she detect some frustration in his voice? "They ask, are you seeing anyone? You say, yes, this incredible, handsome man named Michael."

How could it not come up? Ashley wondered. Michael was right. Wouldn't that have been one of the first questions her parents would have asked? And why hadn't she offered the information?

"No lack of modesty there," Ashley commented.

"Only stating the truth," Michael joked.

"I had brunch with my aunt Kathleen today." Her turn to change the conversation.

"And ...?"

"She said something about how the Art Center named for my mom is struggling financially."

"And you want me to look into it."

"Would you? It would mean so much to her, and me. You do have connections with money."

"Hmmm. Help my fiancée's aunt keep a dance studio and art center financially stable. How much will this cost me, or rather, my grandfather?"

"I don't know. She didn't exactly say they were in trouble, just that they were barely getting by."

"I'll check. Much as I love you, I think my grandfather loves you more. Maybe he could take on another project as patron."

"Thank you, Michael. That would be wonderful. Oh, and about that fiancé part ..."

"I know. Don't say anything until you tell them. But it might be difficult to refrain from showing your family how much I care about you."

"Just be patient a little while longer."

Another secret from her dad, from Ava, and the rest of her family, Ashley thought as she ended the call. Along with the secret she was keeping from Michael. When would all of this secrecy end?

Chapter 14

Up and out of the house by nine. Ashley was back into her routine. The summer dance campers had just arrived when Ashley arrived at the studio. Ashley tried to engage them in conversation, asking names, commenting on their outfits. Wasn't working. What would it take?

"Okay, girls. Time to get started." Danielle called to them. She flashed a smile at Ashley as she rounded up the girls. "Thanks again for yesterday."

Ashley watched as Danielle and Patrice put the girls through their paces, then she sighed. Was it time to admit defeat as far as the young girls were concerned? But no, she was Ashley Reese. She didn't admit defeat.

The young dancers were still at it when she left before noon. She had done a full workout to make up for slacking off the other day. Then home to shower before meeting the other bridesmaids at the dress shop by two.

Her sister, Grace, future sister-in-law, Josie, and a woman she didn't recognize were waiting with flutes of champagne when she arrived.

"Champagne?" the woman attending them asked. Ashley accepted the glass.

"You're drinking Champagne?" Ashley asked Grace.

"Sparkling water." Grace held up her glass and sipped. Ashley should have known. Grace was never one to take chances, unless it involved helping an animal, or a hurt human.

"You remember Josie, don't you?"

"I do. Can't believe that you are the little Josie who was Grace's constant companion. The one who was going to save the world. I don't know how my brother managed to snare you. Wink if you aren't here of your own free will."

"I'm here of my own free will. Your brother can be pretty persuasive." Josie's laughter sparkled, or was that the champagne? Either way, this wasn't the quiet Josie she remembered, playing at make-believe with her sister. Josie had matured in ways Ashley had not imagined.

"I'm aware of that, but his charms usually worked better on cheer-leaders."

Josie laughed and introduced the other woman. "This is Dawn. We've been in school together since I moved to Santa Cruz. We're both studying Environmental Science."

"Someone else to save the world." Ashley smiled and raised her glass to Dawn. "The world needs it."

"Are you ready to try on your dress?" Josie asked.

"Sure." Ashley had already tried on dresses for size in New York. Once the style was agreed upon, it had been sent to Cascade Falls for a fitting. Fortunately, Josie wasn't into frills and lace. From the options, Ashley had chosen an elegant, metallic-blue silk dress that slipped easily over her shoulders, clung nicely to her body, and shimmered as she walked. No strapless dress that risked a dress malfunction, not that Ashley had much in the way of breasts to be exposed. Not like Grace, whose breasts were enlarging with her pregnancy, or Josie's friend Dawn. Ashley didn't have enough breast to hold up a strapless dress.

Breasts … She didn't want to be reminded about breasts.

She was happy that Josie didn't insist on the same dress for each bridesmaid. That only worked if each bridesmaid was a cookie-cutter exact shape and complexion as the other. The dresses were the same color and similar enough to match while allowing for minor differences that meant a lot on diverse body shapes. Grace's dress nicely flowed over her beginning-to-show belly. Each dress reached to their knees. That meant shapely, or not so shapely legs, were exposed. No problem for the three of them.

The seamstress inspected the dresses and marked for any alterations that were needed.

"Now don't gain or lose any weight between now and the wedding," the woman said as she finished marking the dresses.

Then Josie came out to the appropriate round of "oohs" and "ahs." Ashley was glad she hadn't had to go through this for Grace's wedding. She made notes for her own wedding, though. As a prima ballerina marrying into one of the more famous art families in New York, she would not be free to forego certain rituals. There would be expectations.

"You really think it looks good?" Her dress had the same simple elegance as theirs, flowing to the floor to hide the braces on her legs. Ashley had forgotten about Josie's disability. Or maybe, like so much else in high school, she had been oblivious to it. Even so, she remembered Josie had difficulty walking but didn't remember why.

"Do you have the shoes you plan on wearing?" the seamstress asked.

"Yes." Josie slipped on a pair of simple white shoes with enough support to wear with her braces. Ashley caught herself wondering, out of all the women Jacob could have chosen, why Josie? Why not someone with a perfect body? But she also remembered a few occasions when they were teens, when Jacob would reach over and steady Josie, or catch her when she started to fall. Then he went back to doing what he did best, being the annoying prankster. With Josie he had been different. She brought out the best in him. Did Michael bring out the best in her?

"You look elegant and graceful," Ashley told Josie.

"Thank you. That was sweet of you, but you don't have to lie. I know I'll never be graceful, not with these braces."

"I'm not lying. You look beautiful."

"You do, Josie," Grace asserted. "If you knew my sister better, you'd realize she doesn't lie. One of her many faults. She has been known to be pretty blunt. Fortunately, with age, she has learned to be more discerning. Accept the compliment. If she didn't think so, she wouldn't have said anything."

After making a few adjustments, the seamstress gathered the train into a bustle. "It will be your responsibility as bridesmaids to help the bride with her bustle. I'll show you how at the final fitting."

"There's going to be another fitting?" Ashley asked.

"Just to make sure everything is perfect for Josie's special day. Next Thursday."

Ashley reached for another flute of champagne. They clicked glasses and toasted Josie.

Their toast was interrupted by Olivia and her aunt. "I hope you don't mind. Olivia wanted to see your dress and show you hers," Chelsea said.

The girl ran up to Josie. "You look beautiful, Aunt Josie. Just like a fairy princess."

Ashley remembered how Josie and Grace used to pretend to be fairy princesses.

"You think so?" Josie smiled. "You look beautiful too."

Olivia wore a short summer dress made of the same material as the bridesmaids' dresses.

"It'll be even prettier with flowers in your hair. Do you want to wear your hair up or down?" Josie asked her.

"How will you wear your hair, Aunt Josie?"

"Up, like this." Josie pulled her hair up on her head.

"That's how I want my hair."

"We can arrange that."

"Olivia, would you like something to drink? Some orange juice or apple juice?" Ashley approached the girl.

"You're the ballerina from the dance studio."

"Yes, I am."

Olivia frowned at her. "I don't want any."

"Olivia, that's not polite. What do you say?" her aunt corrected her.

Olivia pouted. "No, thank you." Her fingers slipped back into her mouth.

"And what does daddy say about your fingers?"

Her fingers remained in her mouth as she glared at Ashley.

"I'm sorry," Chelsea said. "She hasn't been the same since her mother died, but she's never been so rude."

"That's okay." Ashley assured her then bent down to talk to Olivia.

"Olivia, I know that you don't know me, but your daddy and I used to be friends a long time ago, back in high school. I would like it if we could be friends too."

"No," Olivia stamped her foot. "I don't wanna." She went back to Chelsea and hung onto her dress.

"I don't know what that's about," Chelsea said.

"That's okay," Ashley assured her, but it wasn't. Her heart ached. She had never had a child take such an immediate dislike of her. Maybe she could avoid her, but how? It was going to be a long wedding. Ashley chugged her champagne.

Chapter 15

After the fitting, the women went out for an early dinner at the Crab Shack where they were able to sit outside at a round picnic table and view the lake. A breeze cooled Ashley's face as she watched boats float by, pontoons with friends sharing snacks and drinks, motor boats filled with laughing children pulling other children behind them in inner tubes, jet skis. The sun, hidden behind a cloud, broke through occasionally, sending sparkles across the still waters. Her spirits matched the sky. Cloudy with occasional sun. She wasn't sure how she felt.

Ashley ordered a salad. "What's on the agenda for the next few days?"

"You mean, Ava hasn't told you?" Josie asked.

"She said you had something for us all weekend, but nothing specific."

"Well, tomorrow afternoon Grace has graciously invited us to stay at Blackburn Farm in her new home, where we'll spend the afternoon making table arrangements for the shower on Sunday and the wedding reception."

"Wait. Last I knew, Jacob was making millions with his NBA contract. Why are we doing this?"

"Because it'll be fun, and we are trying to be eco-friendly," Grace told her.

"You do realize who you are talking to? I'm not exactly an artsy-craftsy person."

"Ava warned me you might say that. Don't worry. We have something you can do that won't require any skills," Josie said.

"I hope Ava will be there to keep up my end of this." Ava was a craft queen when she had time. Since Ashley had moved away, Ava had decorated the house with an endless supply of home-made decorations. So much so that Grace had taken to calling her Martha Stewart. She knew what she had promised herself about alcohol intake, but how was she going to get through this without a martini or two? No beer or wine. Too many calories. But a dry martini. Just enough to take the edge off.

"And then what? We aren't doing crafts all weekend are we?" Ashley thought better of ordering a martini. Had to pace herself for the weekend.

"Abel's going to barbecue, big steaks. The groomsmen will be joining us," Grace said. "We'll have homemade potato salad from the local deli, brownies, pie."

Ashley groaned. Oh boy, another orgy of meat.

"Don't worry, though. There'll be veggie burgers and salad for the non-meat eaters. Abel's taking care of it. I made him promise there would be more than meat and potatoes and pie. You know Josie and Dawn are vegetarians too."

"It's better for the planet." Dawn nodded.

"Don't worry. We won't let the guys ruin it for us," Josie assured Ashley. "Saturday we'll be having a spa day. Massages, wraps, facials, mimosas and quiche for breakfast, a light and refreshing salad for lunch. All vegetarian, all organic."

"That's something I can get excited about." Ashley loved massages. With her increase in income, she tried to schedule one each week, along with a mani-pedi. But rarely did she have time to spend a whole day at a spa.

"And Friday night, Magic Mike." Grace pulled out a DVD from her purse.

"You've got to be kidding me," Ashley said.

"Would you rather have male strippers?"

"Hey, I'm a professional dancer. I see men's bodies in all stages of undress all the time. I've seen much better male dancers than anything on that video."

"Lighten up, Ashley. It's just for fun. We don't have to watch it. Or we could watch it and laugh and throw popcorn at the dancers. I thought it was my responsibility as matron of honor to come up with something appropriate for a bachelorette party."

"Between Jacob, Andrew, Abel, Alex and Caleb, I think we'll have enough hot bodies for our own male review." Dawn waved her hand.

"No argument from me," Josie agreed. "How did we end up with such good-looking men?"

"Caleb is coming?" Ashley asked.

"Yes. Caleb and Abel are going to be ushers. They've been invited to the bachelor party. Dante, the other groomsman, isn't able to come until next Friday. He has family commitments. You'll get to meet him then."

"Will other Warriors be attending the wedding?" Dawn asked.

"Not the whole team, but Kevin and a few others."

"I do like a man in a uniform. Who needs strippers when you've got men in shorts running up and down a court?"

"Dawn!" Josie feigned shock.

"Hey, a girl can look. Just so she doesn't touch. Unless, of course she's slipping in a dollar bill or two or more."

Ashley frowned, ignoring the laughter and conversation going on. "Why does Caleb's daughter call you Aunt Josie?" she finally asked. "You aren't related, are you?"

"No, but whenever Jacob and I come home to visit—"

"—Which is never often enough," Grace interrupted.

"— we make a point of catching up with Caleb, especially since his wife died. I don't know why. Olivia seems to like me. I told her to call me Aunt Josie."

"And for some reason she doesn't like me."

"Don't take it personally, Ashley. Who knows what's going on in that little head?" Grace told her.

Don't take it personally? How could she not?

Chapter 16

This was the longest Ashley had been away from New York since she joined The Company. It didn't feel good, being away so long, despite what others had told her. They had insisted it would be good for her. She hadn't wanted a vacation, but she went along with it. Prima ballerinas didn't take vacations. If she was gone too long, someone younger may take her place. But she had been assured by the artistic director that she could be gone two weeks without missing a beat. He didn't say she couldn't check in while she was gone.

Once she was upstairs in her room, Ashley decided to call Audra, her best friend, despite the lateness of the hour. This was New York she was calling. New York didn't wake up until other parts of the country went to sleep. She knew Audra would be up.

"Ashley? Hey everyone, it's Ashley," she heard Audra yell across a noisy room.

"Hi, Ashley." Voices echoed through the phone

"Where are you?" Ashley asked.

"At your favorite Thai fusion restaurant, missing you. Where are you?"

"In my childhood bedroom, surrounded by all my childhood stuff."

"Sorry for you."

"No more sorry than I am for myself. But it's not so bad."

"When are you coming back?"

"I won't be back until a week from Sunday. Remember?"

Ashley heard a noise as Audra's phone was taken out of her hand. "Ashley, you have to get back here," said George, another dancer with The Company.

"What are you talking about, George?"

"Just that we miss you. New York just isn't the same without your sparkling persona."

"Hah, I'm sure New York is still New York."

"And then there's Celeste." Celeste was one of the younger ballerinas in line to take her place.

"Yes?"

"She's in bed with the choreographer of the new ballet for the fall." Ashley's stomach tensed at the suggestion. Just what she feared most. "She's lobbying to dance the lead. Says the part requires someone younger, and so does Marc." Marc was the choreographer.

"That's my part."

"I know, but while you're gone, Celeste and Marc have been working against you. When can you come back?"

When could she? Certainly not this weekend. On Monday she had the biopsy. Could she fly back Monday night, then return on Thursday?

"I'll see what I can do."

"Don't listen to him." Audra's voice came back over the phone. "It's just talk. You know how everybody talks. That part is yours and you know it. Enjoy your time with your family. You deserve it."

She chatted for a while longer with Audra before she had to go. "I miss you girl. Don't let the cow pastures of Cascade Falls, or wherever it is you are, make you forget us and New York."

"Like that would ever happen."

What was she to do now? She knew about Company gossip. Most likely there was nothing to be worried about, but what if there was? She couldn't let her brother down, or the rest of her family. But she also couldn't lose all she had worked for. She needed someone there, on the inside, to plead her case. That someone was Michael.

She was surprised when Michael didn't answer her call. Must be at a company function she told herself. The more she tossed and turned and tried not to think about it, the more convinced she was that she was within inches of losing her position as Prima. She woke up tired from lack of sleep and called Michael. Again, no answer. Maybe he was at work.

She knew not to call Michael at work unless it was an emergency. But this was an emergency.

"Ashley. What's wrong? You know I'm at work."

"I know. I'm sorry to bother you, but it's an emergency."

"Just a minute. I'm in a meeting. Let me get back to my office."

Ashley tried to calm herself while waiting. No luck. Not happening. If anything, she got more upset the longer she waited.

"Okay. Talk to me."

"Celeste—she's trying to replace me."

"What are you talking about? The Company is shut down until time to get ready to go on tour."

"I know. She's trying to get the lead in the new ballet this fall. That's my role, not hers. She's in bed with the choreographer. They're lobbying to get her the part. They say I'm too old. I'm not too old, am I, Michael? I still have good years ahead of me."

"Darling, calm down. Let me check this out. There's no sense in you getting upset until you know it's not just Company gossip. Who told you this?"

"George."

"Okay. I'll check for you. You just relax and have a good time with your family. You know you deserve some time off."

"I wish you were here to hold me and reassure me." Ashley wiped away tears. It was all too much. Being back here in her hometown, the breast biopsy, and now her worst nightmare, losing a coveted role.

"I wish I was too. Don't worry. You know how the gossip network works. If there's any substance to the rumor, I'll use my grandfather's influence to squelch it."

"Thank you, Michael. I knew I could count on you."

"You always can. Now I have to get back to my meeting."

"You'll check this after your meeting?"

"Immediately."

Ashley felt better but wasn't assured. She knew how the gossip network worked at The Company because she had used it herself, to her advantage. But she had to be there to do it.

Ashley grabbed her car keys. "I'm going to practice," she told Ava on her way out, skipping breakfast. A good work-out would help take her mind off everything that was going wrong in her life. First the lump, now this. What next?

She took the stairs to the dance studio two at a time. A good warm-up activity. She was breathing hard as she walked into the studio. Who did she run into, but Olivia?

"Hi, Olivia." Ashley made a feeble attempt to greet the girl.

Olivia frowned, stomped her foot and ran into her classroom. One of these times Olivia's going to stomp on her foot, Ashley thought as Olivia ran off.

She greeted some of the other girls, the one's whose names she remembered. "Hi, Sharon, Mandy, Bree." No response. Why did she feel like she was twelve years old again, trying to gain the attention of the older dancers?

"When is the dance camp done?" Ashley found her aunt in the office.

"Today's the last day. Why?"

"Just wondering." Good, no more Olivia or the other girls after that.

Chapter 17

Grace's new home was a large ranch-style with a porch that extended the length of the front, and a deck extending over a walk-out basement. It was built with every modern convenience, in contrast to the old farm house on the other side of the barn where Abel's grandfather lived.

"It's fabulous," Ashley commented during the tour. "But it doesn't seem like you. You seem more like the old farmhouse type."

"Well, this was Abel's idea. I figure he gave up a good position in Phoenix to move here, so the least I could do was let him have his way about our home."

"Very nice," Ashley added as she examined the immaculate spacious kitchen with center island and metallic appliances. "Do either of you ever use this kitchen?"

"Sometimes." Grace laughed. "But you're right. Between both of our jobs and the farm, we don't spend a lot of time in the kitchen. Most nights we eat with Abel's grandfather. His housekeeper cooks for all three of us. It will be nice if we need it. And it'll work well for the rehearsal dinner."

"You're having the rehearsal dinner here?"

"Why not? We're giving Dad and Ava a break. Remember all the cookouts they've hosted over the years?"

Ashley did remember, how could she not? It was such an important part of her childhood. She continued to explore the kitchen, opening the refrigerator. "A lot of food for someone who doesn't cook."

"That's for tonight. You might say that tonight is the rehearsal for the rehearsal dinner."

The basement featured a living area with a large-screen TV and surround sound.

"For our viewing pleasure," Grace said. There was also an all-purpose room with a long folding table and chairs, set up for making the table decorations. Ava was ready and waiting for them. Ashley scanned the room for drinks and snack. She had skipped lunch in anticipation of a food overload that afternoon and evening.

"No snacks? No champagne?"

"Not until we're done. I don't want any slip ups or mistakes. Here, Ashley, you're in charge of cutting material."

That she could do, though a little champagne might help get through the job quicker. The rest of the group oversaw putting everything together, using a hot glue gun and artificial flower sprigs to decorate votive candle holders.

"Artificial flowers? That doesn't sound like you, Josie," Ashley commented.

"All of the flowers in the church and at the reception will be fresh, locally grown using organic methods. No chemicals," Josie said.

"Now that sounds like you."

"This is just so the decorations last till next week. Then the guests will be able to take them home as a keepsake," Ava explained.

The cloth Ashley cut was being gathered up into fake flowers. How they did it, Ashley didn't know. She just kept cutting. Something more challenging would have helped get her mind off everything, though. Michael hadn't called back yet, but she hadn't expected him to, not till tonight. Maybe not even then. It would take a while, some snooping before he would know anything. Maybe she should have gone back, told everyone she had an emergency to deal with, which was the truth. She would be back for the wedding, only, she hadn't even seen Jacob yet. How could she leave before seeing him? And then what excuse could she tell The Company to explain her early return? She couldn't just come out with accusations without knowing more. This would require some finesse on her part.

No, she was stuck with relying on Michael. Not a bad situation. He'll do okay, just not as good as if she were handling it.

Ashley finished her job cutting material. "Any more to cut?" She stretched her hand, cramped from holding the scissors.

"No," her stepmother told her. "That's it."

"What else can I do?" The rest were intent on their own projects. Ashley picked up a piece of material. "Maybe I can make a flower. Hand over that glue gun."

"No," Ava blurted out, grabbing the gun from her before she could do any damage. "I mean, why don't you go upstairs and see if you can come up with some snacks for us."

"There's cheese to cut up in the refrigerator, a veggie tray with dip, crackers in boxes on the counter," Grace told her.

Ashley looked through the refrigerator, accessing the situation. Beer, wine coolers, champagne. Where was the pitcher of margaritas? Or tonic for gin and tonic? She opened the cupboards, looking for the hard stuff.

"What are you looking for?"

Ashley jumped at the gruff male voice. She turned and faced an older man, eighties most likely, in jeans and a long-sleeved shirt.

"You must be Abel's grandfather, Lamar."

"And you must be one of the bridesmaids. Which one?"

"I'm Ashley. Grace's sister."

"The one from New York? You're some type of fancy dancer."

"Ballerina," Ashley corrected him.

"You still didn't tell me what you're looking for."

"Oh, I was just checking out the drink situation, you know, for tonight."

"No need to look further. Grace doesn't drink and Abel's right fond of beer. Don't suppose that will satisfy you."

"No, that's okay. I'll just help myself to a wine cooler." Ashley looked at the sugar content and put it back down. "Or not. You don't know whether they have any gin or vodka for martinis?"

"Nah, that's fancy drinks."

Ashley grimaced.

"But I do know where Abel keeps the good stuff. Scotch whiskey. Here." He opened a cupboard under the island. "He keeps it here for me so I'm not climbing to get it from the other cupboards. Good Scotch whiskey." Lamar pulled out a brown bottle. Ashley preferred the clears, gin and vodka. Had less calories, but hey, when in Rome …

Lamar poured her a shot. She sniffed it then took a sip. Pretty strong.

"Yep, that's the good stuff." Lamar finished off his shot then put the bottle back in the cupboard. "You know where to find it if you want more. Right now, I've got to get to the barn, check on the horses. You want to come?"

Ashley paused. She was supposed to be getting snacks, but she knew that had just been a ruse to keep her from interfering with the work in progress. She threw back the whiskey and gasped. "Sure. Why not?" No one would miss her.

Pride exuded from the old man as he showed her around the barn and the round riding arena.

"New-fangled stuff my grand daughter-in-law is into. Says if there's no corners, the horse can't get away from you when you train them." He led her to the corral where five horses nuzzled each other and scavenged for grass.

"The big ones, those are the brood mares I purchased. I thought to maybe breed them again, but your sister was against it. Said they were too old, and five horses was all she could handle, until she changed her mind. That one's pregnant."

"That's fantastic," Ashley stated.

"Fantastic? Not awesome? Amazing? I thought that was what you young people use to describe everything."

"I'm not like all those other young people." Why did people always try to put her into a box with everybody else her age? She did not fit in anyone's box. Never would.

Lamar grunted before continuing. "The two little ones, they're the twins. They're a little over a year old. The colt, he's a year and a half, born two Novembers ago. We might try to train him this year. Usually, you wait for them to be two, but he'll be close enough by the end of the summer. All three of those young-uns, they wouldn't be alive today if not for your sister. Heck, the mares, Eleanor and Lady, they wouldn't have made it either."

"I take it you like my sister."

"Naw, but I couldn't have picked a better girl for my grandson if I had picked her myself."

"Abel's a smart man."

"He knows a good one when he sees it, just like his grandfather." Lamar looked over at the horses grazing peacefully in the field. "This was all I wanted, to have horses on my farm once again before I die. I can sit on my porch and watch them any time I want, or go over to my grandson's place and watch them from his fancy deck."

Ashley looked back at Grace's home. The four women were standing on the deck waving at her. They must be finished.

"I guess I better get back to the party. Will you be over later?"

"Won't miss it. One of those steaks has my name on it."

"Fabulous. I'll see you then. Thanks for the tour."

"Fabulous," Lamar grunted and dismissed her with a wave, but Ashley detected a slight smile as he shook his head. At least she still had her knack with older men.

Ashley joined the group on the deck. "How come you didn't tell me your new grandfather was so charming?"

"Because he usually isn't. He must like you," Grace responded.

"I do tend to have that effect on old men. It's helpful when fundraising for The Company."

"I see you've already gotten the tour of the barn," Grace said.

"I can go again if you want." Ashley saw Josie sit down. "Or not. I can stay here with Josie if you want to show Dawn and Ava around."

"Time for me to leave," Ava said. "This party is for you young people. Your dad will be looking for me."

"And if it's okay with everyone else, I'd like to take a short nap before the guys show up," Josie said.

"That leaves Dawn and Ashley. Would you like a tour of the barn?" Grace asked.

"I'd love it," Dawn said.

"And I'll come along for the company," Ashley said.

They made their way down the sloping path to the pasture and barn. It would have been hard on Josie, navigating the uneven terrain.

"I know you've told me this before, but can you tell me again, what is it Josie has?" Ashley asked.

"Charcot-Marie-Tooth Disorder. It's a neurological disorder."

"Is there a cure? A treatment?"

"Not yet. It's progressive. Josie has worked hard to retain the ability she has."

"That's too bad."

"Don't feel sorry for her. Jose wouldn't want that."

"Then what can I do?"

"Just be yourself, or a more considerate version of yourself."

"I can't promise that, but I can try." Being considerate of others wasn't exactly her strong suit.

The guys pulled up around six. Abel had the steaks breathing on the island counter. "You have to let them get to room temperature," he informed her. Not that she wanted to know. Thick slabs of red meat.

Ashley went outside to greet Jacob and his friends. She was amazed at how Jacob had filled out. He was no longer the scrawny, lanky teenager she remembered. "Jacob, is that you?"

Grace came up beside her. "Ashley, let me introduce you to my brother. Oh, wait, he's your brother too."

"Ha ha, smarty," Ashley responded. She and Jacob had both tormented Grace mercilessly as kids. She guessed it was payback time.

Ashley gave Jacob a big hug. Then she stood back as Jacob swooped up Grace in a hug. "Gracie," he said in that tone that used to drive their sister crazy. She didn't seem to mind it anymore. "Good to see you, Graceless."

"You do know Grace's husband is in the kitchen with a big meat cleaver, don't you?" Ashley said.

"I'll let you get away with it, since it's your special event coming up. But if you go too far, I know where the cleaver is," Grace said.

"Where's my beautiful bride-to-be?"

"Catching up on her beauty sleep. She'll be out soon," Grace told him.

"Ashley, you remember Alex, don't you? And this is Andrew. I met him when I was playing for the Santa Cruz Warriors."

"Are you still a Warrior?" Ashley asked.

"Naw, I wasn't good enough to make it out of the minors. Not like your brother. I figured it was time I stopped fooling myself and got a real job."

"You figured it out with a little help from me." Dawn came up and kissed him.

"More than a little help."

Josie appeared on the porch. "The party's out back, not in the driveway," she shouted. Jacob ran up to her and lifted her off her feet in a bear hug.

"I've missed you baby."

"And I've missed you. Now put me down. Carefully."

Jacob set her back down, not letting go till he could tell she was stable. "You heard the woman. The party's out back. Come on in."

The group filed through the house to the deck where Abel had started the grill.

"Is this the party?" Ashley heard Caleb's voice as he came through the kitchen door.

"We've been waiting for you." Jacob fist-bumped with Caleb then gave him a hug.

Caleb did the same with Alex then shook Andrew's hand. "Where's Dante?"

"Couldn't make it. He'll be here Friday," Jacob explained. "I believe you know everyone, except for Dawn."

The introductions being done, Jacob cracked open a beer and handed it to Caleb.

Ashley poured herself a glass of champagne and walked to the edge of the deck. From there she had a panoramic view of the grounds. She could see the horses being led back to the barn. Must be feeding time. She leaned on the railing enjoying the tranquility of the country setting. She felt … almost at peace. Was it possible? She couldn't remember when she had felt this way. Worries about her position being on the line, her health, all faded into the background. She breathed in the goodness.

"Beautiful, isn't it?" Caleb came alongside of her.

"So peaceful."

"Not like New York."

"No, not even remotely." Ashley turned and faced him. "Why does your daughter hate me?"

"What? Olivia? She doesn't hate you."

"Yes, she does. I know that look. She frowns at me and glares. She doesn't respond when I smile at her. You may not realize this, but I'm pretty good with kids, especially little girls." Though you wouldn't know that from the reaction of the girls at the Dance studio, Ashley thought to herself. "You should see them after our matinees. They love me."

"I don't know what's going on with Olivia, but I'm sure she doesn't hate you. She doesn't know you enough to hate you. That takes time and getting to know you."

"Ha ha. Not funny."

"Look, at most she doesn't like you. I don't know why. I don't know what's been going on with that girl since her mother died, but I'm sure if you give her a chance, she'll like you. Why don't you come over, spend some time with us?"

"I don't know. You don't own a gun, do you? Because if so, I think she might shoot me."

"Now who's being funny? I have a gun, but it's kept locked in my closet where she'll never get it."

"Okay. When?"

"Sunday night after the shower?"

"Steak's ready," Abel called.

"Oh boy," Ashley frowned. Time for the meat orgy to begin. "Sunday it is." Ashley agreed and joined the rest of the party.

They ate their meal at the table Abel had set up on the deck so they could enjoy the view. Ashley relished the cool breeze and the company.

"How about a game of volleyball?" Jacob suggested after dinner. "Help us wear off that meal." Abel had a volleyball net set up below on the grass.

Ashley remembered playing volleyball in high school gym class. Not her favorite sport. She had ended up with bruises all up and down her arms from hitting the ball. And knowing how competitive Jacob could be, she imagined getting hit by a spike or elbowed aside in his effort to get the ball.

"Come on, it'll be fun. We'll go easy on you. Abel, Ashley and Grace will be on my team. Alex, Andrew, Caleb and Dawn on the other team. Josie and Lamar can be scorekeepers."

"No volleyball for me," Grace insisted. "Not in my condition."

"Okay, Abel, Ashley and I can take on you four."

"I don't know," Ashley started.

"What's wrong, Ash? Too dainty for a little volleyball?"

Jacob knew just what to say to get to her. He knew her competitive edge too well. "I could run circles around you in high school, and still can. You may be bigger than me, but I'm more flexible and can jump higher."

"We're on. Show me." Jacob accepted the challenge.

Now what? When your livelihood depended on your ability to dance, it wasn't a good idea to put yourself in a position where you could be injured.

"No volleyball for my bridesmaids. I'm not taking any chances on bruises or worse, broken limbs before the wedding." Josie stepped in to stop the game before it began. "Besides, it's time for you guys to leave. Let us get on with our party."

"You heard the bride," Grace said, escorting the men out.

Ashley remained on the deck, watching the remnants of light from the sunset. That was a close one. Saved by the bride.

Chapter 18

The day at the spa was just what she needed. The massage followed by relaxing on a deck with cucumbers on her eyes while her facial solidified, healthy food … fabulous.

The night before had been surprisingly fun too. Even watching Magic Mike wasn't as lame as she had anticipated.

"It's better with the volume off," Dawn said. "Then we can make up our own dialogue."

"It sounds like you've done this before," Ashley stated. They laughed, ate popcorn, threw popcorn at the TV screen and each other, then were in bed by midnight. Not too shabby.

Ashley leaned back and sighed as she felt tension release. She sipped cucumber water through a straw while the facial did its job.

"Tell me, Josie, why didn't you have your wedding in California amid the Redwoods? Grace told me how much you love them. Wedding in Santa Cruz, reception in San Francisco, oh, and the bachelorette party — not that this isn't fantastic."

"We did consider that. We thought seriously about having a small wedding there. Just a few close friends, then having a big party here in Cascade Falls so all of our family could attend."

"What happened?"

"It seems one close friend couldn't make it."

"I told you I would have come. I wouldn't have missed your wedding for anything," Grace defended herself.

"I know. But then if you came, our parents would have wanted to come, and other family members, and before we knew it, our small, environmentally friendly wedding in the Redwoods would have been a massive wedding. Neither of us wanted that."

"So, your solution was having everything here in Cascade Falls," Ashley said.

"What's wrong with Cascade Falls?" Grace asked.

"Nothing, it's just, it's Cascade Falls, and San Francisco is—"

"San Francisco," Dawn and Josie said together.

"Right." Ashley sighed and took another sip of cucumber water. "How did you and Jacob…? I mean, you weren't exactly friends when you were kids. How did you end up snagging him?"

"It was him that snagged me. I didn't like him as a kid. He was so mean to my best friend here, always teasing her and picking on her."

"That was Jacob." Ashley and Grace agreed.

"But then, I got to know him better. He can be really sweet."

"That I've yet to see, but I'll take your word for it." Ashley finished off her water. Then it was time for their wraps and mani-pedis followed by tea.

"And for tonight," Josie got their attention as they finished off tea time at the spa.

"Tonight? You mean there's more?" Ashley asked.

"There sure is." Josie paused for effect. "Tonight, ballroom dancing lessons."

"What? Who are we going to dance with?" Grace asked.

"The groomsmen, silly. Look, I know I can't dance, except maybe to rock back and forth with Jacob, but we still want to have a bridal party dance. We have the dance studio reserved and ballroom dance instructors signed up. My parents and Jacob's parents will be there too, for the mother-son and the father-daughter dance. I want to show off my bridal party. After all, we have a world-acclaimed dancer in our midst. Why not use it?"

"Why not?" Ashley agreed. She wasn't sure about this, but she did like showing off, so why not?

They arrived at the dance studio at six. The dance instructors were somewhat cheesy, but what did she expect? She had danced with the best. They did a demonstration to start with, then asked Josie to pair everyone.

"Okay," Josie said. "Listen up. Grace will be dancing with Alex, the best man, Dawn with Andrew, and Ashley with Dante. Since Dante isn't here, Caleb will stand in for him. I'll dance with my dad. Jacob will dance with his mom."

Ashley hadn't noticed Caleb enter the room. He slipped up behind her.

"I believe this is our dance."

"I can't seem to get away from you. You're everywhere."

"Is that a bad thing?"

"Depends. I'll see how you dance."

"It's not every day a guy gets to dance with a world-class ballerina. I'm not sure I'll be able to keep up."

"I'm only as good as my partner. Or, on second thought, I can be better than my partner, often am, but a good partner does make a difference."

"No pressure here." Caleb took her hand and placed his arm around her waist.

"None at all." Ashley placed her free hand on his shoulder. Caleb was ragged at first, but not entirely clueless.

"You forget, my wife was a dancer. She taught me a few things," he said.

"More than a few." As they grew more comfortable dancing together, Ashley asked, "I see Geri seems interested in you. Are you an item?"

"No, though she would like that. You know how it goes."

"No, I don't."

"A man becomes eligible and all of the single women, and sometimes their mothers, start showing up at your door with casseroles, or in Geri's case, pizza and a six-pack."

"I thought that was for older widowers."

"No, any widowers. Anyway, I'm not interested. I'm not ready. You don't get over the loss of a wife in a year. Besides, I have Olivia to consider."

"I imagine there are a lot of single women sad to know that."

Josie sat down part way into the lesson. Towards the end, she danced with Jacob while their parents danced together.

Her dad and Ava came alongside of Ashley and Caleb.

"Looking good," Caleb said to them.

"You too," her dad winked at her. Now what was he up to? Maybe it was time she told everyone about Michael, but how?

Chapter 19

Jacob caught her on her way out the door Sunday night. "Hey, sis, where are you going? I thought we could hang out."

"Where's Josie?"

"Resting after the big weekend. So how about catching up, you and me?"

"Sorry, Jacob. I have somewhere to go, but I won't be late." She didn't know why she didn't tell him where she was going. No, correct that. She knew why. She didn't want the knowing winks and smiles. She and Caleb were just friends. She wanted to be friends, or at least be tolerated by his daughter.

You could solve this problem, an inner voice told her. She knew what she could—should—do. Tell them about Michael.

Tell them about Michael? Why is that so difficult? Maybe because it would bring her New York world into her hometown world. Maybe she wanted to keep them separate. Maybe it was nice to feel like a teenager for a while. If she wanted to prolong that feeling, who was she hurting?

She had talked to Michael briefly that afternoon, slipping out of the bridal shower to do so. He had some further checking to do but assured her she had nothing to worry about. Nothing to worry about? Easy for him to say. But she took him at his word. What choice did she have? She almost wished he had told her there was a problem. Just the excuse she needed to leave early and go back to the life she knew in New York. Instead, duty called. She had to hang up and get back to the bridal shower.

The shower had been okay, in a mid-western, small-town way, if you like such things. Watching Josie open presents — it wasn't her idea of a good time, but as long as her future sister-in-law was happy ... and she was from what Ashley could tell. Olivia had attended, clinging to Chelsea the whole time and eyeing Ashley suspiciously.

Ashley pulled up to the small house on the other side of town. A small two-bedroom in a quiet neighborhood, mostly older couples with similar small houses. It must have been all Caleb could afford. But it had a garage, one Caleb had made into a makeshift studio. She wondered what his neighbors thought of his band.

"Hey, Ashley. We're out here," Caleb called from his fenced-in back yard.

There was a slide and swing set and a princess playhouse. Olivia was dressed in a makeshift princess outfit.

"Her aunt's doing." Caleb followed her gaze.

"You didn't seem quite the fairy-princess guy. Nice yard. Have you considered getting a dog?"

"Shhh. Olivia already has that idea. She doesn't need fuel for the fire."

"Hmmm, could be a way to get her to like me."

"And alienate her father."

"Just a thought."

"I told Olivia no dog till she was old enough to take care of it. What I really mean is, I need the time and energy to take care of one. Maybe in a year or two. Right now, it's all I can do to keep going."

Ashley remembered Lucky, how he had helped her through her mom's illness and death. She thought better of saying more.

"Olivia, come here. We have a guest."

"Who?" Her head popped out the window. When she saw Ashley, it went back in.

"I'll get her." Caleb went over to the playhouse. "Olivia, come out."

"I don't want to."

"We have a guest. Don't be rude."

"Why is she here?"

"Because I invited her. Come out and say hi, then you can go back to your play."

Olivia came out, pouting. "Hi," she said, then ran back inside.

"No, not enough. Come over here and talk to her."

Ashley shook her head. She wanted to tell him to let her be, but she didn't want to interfere with his parenting.

Olivia slowly walked over to where Ashley sat. "Hi."

"Hi, Olivia. I love your princess dress."

"My aunt got it for me. She said it used to be my mother's."

"That's nice of your aunt."

"Can I go back now?" Olivia asked her dad.

He nodded yes.

"Let it go," Ashley told him. "You can't force this." She stood up. "Let me see what I can do."

"I'll get us something to drink. Beer?"

"No. I'm detoxing. Water."

Ashley sauntered to the playhouse, looking sideways into the window. Olivia peeked out the window then went back in.

Ashley knocked on the door. "Olivia, can I come in?"

"No," the small voice resounded in the house.

"Okay. How about we just talk?"

"Go away."

Ashley wanted to go away. But she wasn't going to be defeated by a girl one third her size.

"You know, I always wanted a playhouse when I was a little girl."

No response.

"But my mom was so busy at the dance studio, and we were always there with her. You might say I grew up at the dance studio."

No response.

"I saw you dance, Olivia. You're good."

Olivia opened the door and stood in the doorway, blocking any entrance. "I know what you're doing, and it won't work."

"What am I doing?"

"You're trying to make friends with me."

"Would that be so bad?"

"I want you to go away."

"I'm not going away, not right away anyway. I'll be going back to New York next week. Can't we be friends till then?"

"You're going away?"

"Yes, but I'll be back to visit. I would like it if we were friends."

"I don't want you to come back."

"Why?"

"Because then my mommy won't come back." Ashley's heart ached as Olivia crossed her arms in front of her and defied Ashley to disagree.

"Oh, sweetheart. Your mommy isn't coming back." Ashley got down face to face with Olivia. "Didn't your daddy tell you?" She tried to hug her.

"Don't say that. You don't know. My mommy is coming back!" she yelled and slammed the door.

Ashley looked back at Caleb. She got up and joined him, taking a swig of his beer.

"Maybe I will take that beer. Did you hear that?"

"The last part of it. How could I not?"

"You told her that her mother wasn't coming back, didn't you?"

"I did, but what she heard, I don't know. Do you think I should talk to her?" He put the beer down on the picnic table and stood up.

"Not now. Give her some time. But how am I involved in this? How is my presence keeping her mom from coming home?"

"I don't know. Maybe it has something to do with you being a dancer, like her mom." Caleb shrugged then sat back down on top of the picnic table.

"Maybe, but that doesn't make sense." Ashley joined him, sitting down by his side as they both looked at the playhouse.

"Grief doesn't make sense. It just is," Caleb sighed.

"Maybe I should go. Give you time to talk to Olivia."

"No, don't go. I know how to get Olivia out of her playhouse. Watch." He walked over to the playhouse. "Olivia, you want to get some ice cream?"

"Is she coming with us?" Olivia peeked out the window.

"Yes."

"Then no." Her head darted back inside.

"Come on. You don't have to talk to her. We'll get your favorite, chocolate-coated ice cream cone."

The door opened and the small figure came out. "I don't have to talk to her?"

"You don't have to talk to anyone you don't want to."

"Okay." She took his hand but eyed Ashley suspiciously.

"There's an ice cream shop within walking distance," Caleb told her. "Then maybe we can go to the park."

"No, I don't want to go to the park," Olivia said.

"But you love the park," Caleb said.

"I don't want to go with her." Olivia glared at Ashley.

"Okay. We don't have to go to the park," Caleb agreed.

They sat in a booth in the small store. Caleb and Ashley talked while Olivia worked on her cone, breaking off the hardened chocolate and putting it on her napkin to eat later.

"That's how I used to eat my ice cream," Ashley said. "I saved the best, the chocolate, for last."

"Not me," Caleb said. "I go for the best first."

Olivia ignored them.

"Ashley, will you be dancing in *The Nutcracker* this winter?" Caleb asked.

"Every year. I'll be the Sugar Plum Fairy."

"Olivia's mom loved *The Nutcracker*. Listened to it every Christmas. She would dance around the house to the music. They always took a group of students from the dance studio to a performance. They were never big enough to do their own production."

"That's a shame. Every ballet student should have the chance to dance in *The Nutcracker* sometime. Don't you think so, Olivia?"

"My daddy said I don't have to talk to you."

"You don't." Ashley looked at Caleb. "Maybe you could come to New York at Christmas and see *The Nutcracker*."

"That sounds like a great idea. What do you think, Olivia? Would you like to go see *The Nutcracker* in New York?"

"Can I see the tree in Rockefeller Plaza and go to the Bronx Zoo?"

"How do you know about that?" her dad asked.

"I do watch TV, Daddy."

"You can do whatever you want. I'll arrange it," Ashley told her.

"Okay." Olivia gulped the last bite of cone, then slowly ate the pieces of chocolate. "Can we go to the park now?"

Ashley looked at Caleb and smiled.

"Of course." Caleb wiped chocolate and ice cream off Olivia's fingers and face.

Olivia jumped down and rushed to the door. This time when she took her dad's hand, she reached for Ashley's hand as well, walking between them.

Chapter 20

Ashley stayed at Caleb's and helped him put Olivia to bed.

"I don't know what we did, but it worked. At least she doesn't hate me," Ashley said as they shut the bedroom door.

"It's what you did. I told you it was just a matter of time. You were bound to win her over."

"But I wonder what she meant by saying if I didn't leave her mother wouldn't come back?"

"I don't know. I'll try to find out. You want a beer?"

"No. Time for me to leave. I have to be up early tomorrow." Her mouth said she had to leave, but her feet resisted. "This was nice, spending time with Olivia, with you."

"We should do it again."

"We should. When I have a free night—"

"—When you have a free night," they said together and laughed.

"Now I really have to go."

"Tomorrow? How about tomorrow?"

"Can't. I must spend some time with my family. I've hardly talked to Jacob since he got home."

"Then Tuesday?"

"Tuesday. Okay."

Caleb walked her to her car. He leaned in as if he was going to kiss her then they heard a small voice and little head appeared in an upstairs window.

"Daddy."

"Olivia. Guess I better go." He slowly pulled back as she opened her car door and sat down.

"You better go." She shut the door and rolled the window down. "Tuesday."

What was she thinking? She'd be leaving soon. Why even start something that would have to end before it began? And then there was Michael. Michael! That's right, her fiancé. She needed to talk to him. How could she have forgotten him?

Jacob and her dad were watching the baseball game when she arrived home. Michael would have to wait a little longer.

"Dad, is the Arts Center in trouble financially?" she asked during a commercial break.

"Not any more than it usually is. Why?"

"Aunt Kathleen seemed to think it was."

"Oh, she did?" Her dad and Jacob both laughed.

"What's so funny?"

"Aunt Kathleen will do anything to keep Mom's legacy going, including enlisting you to help her fundraise," Jacob said.

"It was more about getting me to take over so she could retire."

Her dad nodded his head. "That too. Not only is it your mom's legacy, it's your aunt Kathleen's baby. She's dedicated over twenty years of her life to Joy's Center."

"Do you think it will have to close if Aunt Kathleen retires?"

"Hard to say. She might sell the building. Originally, any money from the sale was to go to you kids. I told her you are financially stable, so keep the money."

"What about Chloe?"

"She can't afford to buy your aunt Kathleen out. And there still would be the issue of finding someone to either take over the dance studio or the direction of the Center. Chloe can't do both."

"There's no one else that could step into Chloe's position?"

"At one point, we thought Stacey, Caleb's wife, would do that. But now, no."

Olivia's mom. Could that be …? "It would be a shame to have it go out of the family."

"Yes, it would. I think your aunt Kathleen, well, all of us, have been hoping that maybe someday …" her dad's head turned slightly towards her and he hesitated before saying, "maybe you would move back and take over running the center."

"My life is in New York."

"It is now, but someday …" her dad's voice trailed off.

"Yeah, it's like eventually I'll have to retire from playing pro ball," Jacob stated.

"What will you do then?" Ashley asked.

"I don't know. Coach? Or maybe I'll join Josie in her crusade to save the environment."

"Nothing says you can't do both," their dad said.

"Or you could run the Center," Ashley suggested.

Both men laughed.

"Ash, how much do you know your brother? I know you haven't seen him in a long time, but even you must realize running an arts' center is not his gift."

"A gal can ask. What's wrong with asking? And, Jacob, what better way to spend your basketball money than supporting our mother's legacy?"

Her dad and brother continued to laugh.

"You're sounding like the director of the center already. Seems you're a natural," her dad stated. Ashley frowned at the suggestion.

"Not that I'm opposed to the idea of helping out financially," Jacob said. "I've already offered, though now I have Josie to consider."

"I hope you don't blame your aunt Kathleen for trying to recruit you to replace her. It isn't only about keeping the Arts' Center in the family. It's also about seeing more of you."

"I get it, Dad. You don't have to keep hinting about that."

"Who's hinting? I thought I was being pretty direct."

"Along with Grace and everybody else in the family." Ashley stood up. "But maybe there is something I can do to help the Arts' Center, financially that is. Goodnight." She gave her dad a hug. "I've got to be up early tomorrow."

"That's right. What are you and Ava doing tomorrow morning?" Jacob asked.

"Just a girls' day in Ann Arbor. Can't a girl spend some time with her stepmother without getting grilled?" she snapped.

"Whoa, sorry I asked."

And she was sorry she had reacted that way, but didn't say so.

"Remember, schedule some time for me," Jacob added.

"Tomorrow afternoon?"

"I have to check with Josie. I'll let you know."

"You sound like a married man already." Their dad slapped him on the back and laughed, then went back to the baseball game.

Ashley texted Michael before going to bed. "Sorry. Early morning tomorrow. Will call tomorrow night." She included the appropriate emojis then clicked send. Michael would have to wait. Her life was on hold.

Chapter 21

The alarm sounded at six. Ashley crawled out of bed. This was really happening. She showered and dried her hair before coming downstairs at seven. Ava and her dad were in their customary places, drinking coffee. Ava jumped up, put her coffee cup on the counter and went for her purse.

"So, a girls' day out?" her dad said as she waited for Ava. "You two have fun."

"We will." Ava kissed him and they went out the door.

"You still haven't told your dad?" she asked as she backed the car out of the garage.

"No, and don't you start in on me."

"I won't. But the problem with secrets is that sometimes they take on a life of their own and before you know it, when you want to tell, you can't."

"I thought you said you weren't going to start in on me."

"Okay. No more." Ava pulled the car onto I-94 to Ann Arbor. "Where are we going? The hospital?"

"No, the doctor's office. It's going to be an out-patient procedure at his office. I thought you knew that."

"I guess I did."

"It's not like you to not have everything mapped out days ahead of time."

"It's also not like me to be keeping secrets from my husband."

Ashley didn't respond. Her stepmom had her there. Still, it wasn't like Ava not to be prepared for every possibility, even if she had to sneak around to do it. Was something else going on?

"What do you want to do afterwards?" Ava asked.

"I don't know. Haven't thought that far."

"I figured as much. I thought brunch at Zingermann's in downtown Ann Arbor and then shopping. There are so many great small stores downtown. We could easily spend hours exploring."

Now that sounded like her stepmom. "You're the driver. Whatever you want."

The procedure only required a local anesthetic. She lay face down in some machine that helped pinpoint the questionable spots. There was the small lump and the dense material. The doctor numbed her left breast then removed tissue from several spots. The procedure was over in less time than it took to numb her.

"Where do we go from here?" Ashley sat up on the exam table with a flimsy paper covering wrapped about her. She looked over at Ava who had been invited back to be with her.

The doctor stood at eye level and talked to her. "We send the samples to the lab. The lump looks benign, the other needs a closer look. Both look good. No reason for alarm. My office will contact you as soon as we have results. We'll fax the information to your doctor in New York, then he'll determine where we go from there. Sound good?"

Sound good? "A clean bill of health would sound better, but I guess I don't have any other options." She expected Ava to say something. She didn't. Again, not like her.

The doctor looked at both women. "Okay. We'll be in touch."

The nurse came in with instructions on how to care for the incision. "Keep it covered until tonight. Other than that, nothing special. Though we do advise you to take it easy for the rest of the day."

"That won't prohibit shopping?" Ava asked.

"Not at all." The nurse smiled and left Ashley to get dressed.

Both were silent on the drive downtown to Zingermann's. They placed their orders, waited for them at the counter then took their trays outside and found seats. A cool, mid-morning breeze blew past them. Ava shivered and pulled the light sweater she was wearing tighter.

"Ava, what's wrong?" Ashley broke the silence.

"What do you mean?"

"Even I can tell you aren't acting like yourself."

"Let's see. One daughter is married and expecting a baby, my first grandchild. Our son is getting married, and the other daughter has a lump in her breast. What's wrong with that? Nothing, but it is a lot going on."

"Ava, tell me." Ashley knew she wasn't exactly the best people person, but when it came to her stepmom, she could tell when something was wrong.

"Okay. But you can't tell anyone." Ava took a deep breath and pushed away her half-eaten quiche. "I haven't been feeling like myself the past few years. Tired. Your dad thinks I'm tired from working too hard. Maybe that's right, but it doesn't account for how tired I've been."

"You haven't seemed tired."

"Because I'm not working. During the school year though, it's all I can do to make it through the day. Your dad wants me to retire. I'm too tired at night to cook, do the laundry, all the things I always did."

"Maybe he's right. Why don't you retire?"

"But, if I retire, what will I do? You kids are gone. My life has been teaching."

"You'll have a grandbaby to spoil."

At the mention of a grandbaby, Ava started crying.

"Ava, what's wrong? Aren't you happy about Grace's baby?"

"I'm happy, ecstatic. It's just, the doctor is doing some tests. He thinks it might be MS – multiple sclerosis."

Multiple sclerosis? Ashley didn't know much about MS but she knew it wasn't good. "But he doesn't know."

"No, he doesn't. It's hard to diagnose. But, if it is, it'll mean no holding my grandbaby. Not being able to play with the baby as it grows."

"But you don't know that. And even if it is the case, you won't lose your physical ability immediately."

"No. It could take years. I could have a lot of good years ahead of me. It's just the thought of retiring and then, not being able to care for my grandchild. It's overwhelming. The children at school have been my life." Ava stirred her coffee but didn't take a sip as it grew cold in the morning air.

"When will you know?"

"I have a doctor appointment next Thursday, when everything from the wedding is done. When it's back to normal."

"Dad doesn't know?"

"I haven't told him yet. I didn't want to spoil Jacob's wedding. Besides, we don't know."

"That's right, like we don't know about me." Ashley finished her fruit cup. "It seems I'm not the only one in this family with a secret." She smiled at Ava as she wiped away her tears and laughed. "We'll be secret buddies, like a secret club. Pinky swear?"

"Pinky swear." They crossed pinkies. "I guess we have reasons to pray."

Ashley frowned and started to open her mouth when Ava stopped her.

"Don't worry. I'll pray for both of us. And now, we have some shopping therapy ahead of us."

Ashley chose to ignore Ava's comment about prayer. It was just how her stepmother was. You have to make allowances sometime. Ava was well aware of her thoughts on the subject. When you don't believe in God, to whom can you pray?

Chapter 22

They were home by three, "to beat the rush hour traffic," Ava said. The older woman slipped upstairs for a nap while Ashley sought her brother. She found him on the back deck, scrolling on his phone.

"Where's Josie?" Ashley sat down next to him with an open bottle of water.

"Hanging with Grace. She says she has the rest of her life to be with me, and only these two weeks to be with her best friend."

"Smart woman." Ashley took a swig of water. "How did you two end up together? I mean, it's not like she's exactly your type. I always thought you were more into blonde, cheerleaders. Not that I have anything against Josie."

"You really don't know Josie that well. She's the smartest person I know and so dedicated and clever and talented …"

Ashley bent her head and stared at him.

"Okay. That was my type, until Josie. But you know, I always had a soft spot for her. I think I knew back then, when we were kids, that we would end up together."

"You sure took your time. I do remember times when you were actually kind to Josie."

"You noticed when you weren't barricaded in your own world."

"Hey, being a dancer is a demanding career."

"It wasn't just about being a dancer."

"Was I really that bad?"

"Worse."

Ashley splashed water from her bottle on him.

"Hey. You know I can give worse than I get." Jacob reached for her water bottle and poured the remainder of her bottle over her head.

"Truce, truce," Ashley screamed. "I thought all teenagers were basically self-centered."

"Self-centered didn't begin to describe you."

Ashley flinched at his bluntness. "I'm sorry."

"Don't be. I admired your drive, though I never would have admitted it then. If I had had half of your ambition, I would have been playing pro ball out of college. As it is, I wasted a number of years, playing around, not focusing. Josie helped me focus."

"Good for her. Where are you going on your honeymoon?"

"New Zealand."

"I've heard it's beautiful there. Lots of islands, natural habitat."

"We aren't exactly going as tourists."

"No?"

"We will do some of the touristy things, but then we'll be working on one of the islands with the Island Restoration Project. Josie's idea. She's been volunteering with them since she moved to Santa Cruz."

"Wow, she has had quite the influence on your life. Giving up your honeymoon. What will you be doing?"

"Ridding the island of invasive species. What about you? No man in your life?"

"There is one, Michael. He's coming to the wedding."

"Sounds serious. Bringing him to meet the family. Is this the one to get you to hang up your ballet slippers?"

"Hardly. Anyone who asks that would automatically be out of my life."

"Just wondering if Ms. Ashley Reese, prima ballerina, would ever settle down?"

Ashley turned aside to check her phone. Who was calling now? Aunt Kathleen. She was glad for the excuse to avoid Jacob's question. She stood up and moved away from him to take the call.

"Ashley, how would you like to go to Detroit and see Letty's dance studio?"

"I'd love it. Can it be arranged?"

"Already is. I'll pick you up tomorrow morning at eight." She would like to see Letty and her studio, but what was Aunt Kathleen up to now?

Ashley went into the kitchen and came out with two bottles of water. "Can I trust you with this?" she asked before handing one to Jacob.

"As much as I can trust you."

They were still there chatting when their dad came home.

"Good to see my kids home again." He sat down across from them. "The only thing better than having two of my kids under the same roof, is having all three of them."

"Are Grace and Abel coming over?" Ashley asked.

"Just Grace. Abel had to go to Chicago on business. She'll be bringing my soon-to-be new daughter."

Ava joined them, fresh from her nap, followed by Grace and Josie.

"Just like when we were kids," Jacob said. "Josie was as much a part of the family then as she is now."

"Marrying you is just a formality," Dad said.

"That's right. I'm just marrying you for your family." Josie smiled, reached for Jacob's water bottle, took a drink then handed it back to him. She laughed as Jacob pulled her on his lap and kissed her. They seemed to be the perfect couple. Ashley sighed.

Jacob insisted on clearing the table and taking care of the dishes after dinner, telling his dad and Ava to sit down. "You cooked. Ashley and I can clean up. You stay here with Grace and Josie."

"Hey, whose idea is this?" Ashley asked.

"Come on, sis. Isn't it about time we paid Dad and Ava back for all those meals they fixed for us over the years? You do remember how to do dishes, don't you?"

"I'm not exactly living in the lap of luxury, like some NBA stars I know. I still have to do my own cooking and cleaning."

"NBA stars, who would that be? Last I knew I was still doing my own cooking and cleaning too."

"Yeah, like ordering pizza or burgers from Shake Shack," Grace said.

"You want in on this? You could help us too, Gracie," Jacob said.

"Just like old times," Ava said.

"Remind me again why I missed this?" their dad asked.

"You know you love having us around," Jacob said.

"That I do. I love it even more when you clean up."

Ashley helped Jacob clean up the kitchen and start the dishwasher.

"Now about that volleyball game—" Jacob began.

"You need more than one person to play volleyball."

"Maybe so, but not for badminton."

"Hmmm," Ashley thought. There was a lot less chance of getting hurt playing badminton than volleyball, though there was the chance of catching her foot in one of the many uneven spots in the yard and possibly spraining an ankle. Still, it would be exercise. And it didn't require brute force to win. She could beat Jacob at this. "You're on."

Ashley slipped out of her sandals and put on a pair of canvas tennis shoes while Jacob set up the net. The shoes were light but offered support and protection to her feet.

When she went back outside, her dad, Ava, Grace and Josie were sitting in lawn chairs alongside the volleyball net to watch the competition.

"Care to make this more interesting?" Jacob asked.

"I'm listening."

"When I win, you will have to come to San Francisco for a game of my choosing."

"Oh, when you win? When I win, you will have to come to New York to watch me in a performance with The Company." Ashley knew it would be a lot harder on Jacob, watching her in a production, than her watching him play basketball. While she had attended basketball games in high school, Jacob had to be dragged to her recitals. He fidgeted until the finale. Jacob would rather eat nails than sit through a ballet.

"And you'll have to take me with you. I'd love to see Ashley dance," Josie said from the sidelines.

"No chance of that happening. I've got this," Jacob responded. "Deal." They shook hands on it, then began to play. Both were out of practice. Jacob tried slamming the birdie only to have it get caught repeatedly in his racket.

"Ease up on it, Jacob," his dad yelled.

Ashley missed the birdie at first until she got a feel for it again. Like riding a bike or driving a car. She still had it. She lightly tossed the birdie back at Jacob, who was having trouble hitting the birdie with a racket.

"How about I just use my hand?" he suggested.

"Nah. You use the racket or forfeit the game."

They both got better as the game progressed, staying within single digits of each other. Ashley was one point away from winning when Josie came over to Jacob, took the racket out of his hand and kissed him, making him lose the game as the birdie sailed pass him.

"Hey, what was that for?" Jacob protested.

"It's about going to New York to see your sister perform."

"I didn't have to lose for that to happen. We could have gone anyway."

"Would we? Now you have to go." Josie smiled, hit the birdie back to Ashley. "I call that the game."

"Not fair. I demand a rematch."

"That you can. But for now, it's time for me and Grace to leave. Walk me to the car. What you do after I leave is up to you."

"Only you can get away with this." Jacob leaned in for another kiss.

"I know." Josie kissed him back then led him away.

While Jacob walked Josie and Grace to Grace's car, Ashley escaped to her room to call Michael. "I'm so sorry. You have no idea how crazy it has been here."

"I look forward to finding out this weekend."

"That will be even worse. Right now, it's immediate family, my brother and sister, parents, grandparents, Aunt Kathleen. Come Friday a host of cousins and their kids will descend upon the sleepy town of Cascade Falls. Are you sure you're up for it?"

"Are you trying to scare me away?"

Ashley could see his smile in her memory. She held onto that memory, needed to, lest she lose herself. "No, not at all. I wish you were here to keep me sane. Did you find out anything else?"

"It's nothing more than the usual gossip and backstabbing."

"Nothing to be worried about?"

"I didn't say that. Celeste is maneuvering to be the next prima. That's to be expected. You know that. Nothing I can't handle for you till you get back."

Yes, she did know about that. She knew about the intrigue that was part of The Company. She remembered how hungry she had been for the position before she got it. How she had catered to choreographers, managers, and patrons, until she had found the ultimate patron in Michael's grandfather and through him, had found Michael. Not that she could ever take anything for granted. There was always another young dancer waiting to take her place. Sometimes something as arbitrary as a word of complaint or criticism could lead to a dancer being removed. Michael and his grandfather helped, but even they couldn't assure she would keep the position.

Directors and choreographers could be very picky—she's too tall, too short, too skinny, too fat, too blond, too flat-chested, too buxom. Any physical flaw, real or unreal, could deny a dancer a role.

Ashley knew of a dancer who had made a casual criticism of a choreographer that had been overheard and led to her not being cast in a coveted role in his production. Ashley was not known for watching her tongue, though she was getting better with Michael's help. Maybe he was good for her, helping her be better …

"You know there's only so much grandfather's money can do," he would remind her.

His grandfather, however, seemed to like it when she blurted out her opinions. She just needed to be aware of who might overhear what she said.

And then there were those other adversaries of all dancers. Time and her body. No amount of money could stop the passage of time or keep her safe from dance-related injuries. Even the most careful dancer can slip, break a bone, sprain an ankle, tear a tendon.

Male dancers had it easier. For one thing, they had less competition. They also didn't have to sacrifice their childhood the way women dancers did. They could start dancing later and still succeed. And no pointe shoes. Much as she loved dancing *en pointe*, it did hurt—not just her feet, but her whole body. And men were paid more than women. If she didn't love dance so much, she never would have tolerated such a sexist profession.

But she did love dancing. Even for this short length of time it was hard to go without performing. Ordinarily, when The Company went dark between seasons, she went on the road, joined other companies. Anything to keep dancing and keep money coming in. She loved the music, the moment when everything came together, the lights, the costumes, and the applause. Dancing was her life, just like teaching was her stepmother's life. She gazed at her old ballet slippers, barely visible in the dim room. So many memories.

What would she do if she didn't dance? She didn't want to think about it, yet the limits on her shelf life as a ballet dancer forced her to look beyond. Did she want to be a choreographer? Did she want to train other dancers? Manage a dance studio? Or stay on at The Company in some capacity? Maybe running Joy's Center for Healing and the Arts wasn't such a far-fetched idea. She quickly pushed that thought aside, put it in a box and shoved it to the far reaches of the attic in her mind.

"Thank you, Michael. I knew I could count on you." And she could. One of the few things in her life she could count on. That, and her family—much as she hated to admit it.

Chapter 23

Another early morning. Ashley texted Caleb to let him know where she was going. "Not sure when I'll be back. I'll let you know when I'm on my way home."

"No prob," Caleb texted back. No problem. Caleb was low maintenance. She liked that. Not demanding like some of her suitors had been. Not that Caleb was anything but a friend.

Chloe had arranged to take the day off from the dance studio to come along.

"Now that summer dance camp is over, I don't have any classes requiring my attention. Thanks for letting me tag along," she said from the back seat of Aunt Kathleen's car. It reminded Ashley of driving to Irish dance lessons years ago, only then she had been the one sitting in the back seat of Aunt Kathleen's car while Chloe and Aunt Kathleen chatted in the front seat.

"Thank you again for meeting with my advanced class. The girls loved it. They are excited about tomorrow. It's all they keep talking about. They want to know if you will dance with them next time."

"That could be arranged."

Ashley didn't know whether having Chloe along was good or not. Would Chloe keep Aunt Kathleen from trying to get her to take over the Art Center? Or would the two of them try to double-team her?

"Will we get to see Aunt Sara while in Detroit?" she asked. Her Aunt Sara had moved to Detroit years ago, while her mother was still alive. Ashley had stayed with her while training with Letty to get into Juilliard.

"Of course. She'll be joining us at Freedom House then going to lunch with us." Freedom House was named for the slaves who had passed through on their way to Canada and freedom. It had once been part of the Underground Railroad. The building had been preserved for historical value as well as hosting Letty's dance studio.

Aunt Kathleen dropped Chloe and Ashley off while she looked for parking. Letty met them on the steps with warm hugs.

"Girlfriend! Ashley, so good to see you. I've got a real prima ballerina visiting my studio!"

"Would never have happened without you."

"Chloe helped too." Letty nodded in Chloe's direction.

"That she did."

"I was just wise enough to recognize when I had taken a student as far as I could." Chloe said. She had danced on Broadway, but never made it beyond a few chorus lines. When she became pregnant, she had moved to Cascade Falls to live with her grandfather and started teaching at the dance studio.

Letty was a former student of Ashley's mother. She had helped at Joy's Studio of Dance, taking over operation after Joy's death. Letty had been instrumental in setting up Joy's Center for Healing and the Arts, along with Aunt Kathleen. When Letty made it into the Alvin Ailey dance company in New York, Chloe took over her position running the dance studio. When a broken bone side-lined Letty from dancing, she came back to Michigan, and settled in Detroit, establishing Freedom House with Aunt Sara's help. Since then, Freedom House had become known as one of the premiere venues for experimental dance, but also for training young dancers for New York.

The building that had been in disrepair when Letty started was fully restored to its original beauty. Like Joy's Center, the first floor was a hub for small businesses, only there was a social justice focus, in line with Letty's second passion after dance. There was a museum featuring Underground Railroad memorabilia and other artifacts related to that part of Detroit's history. A legal services clinic that specialized in immigration services and a health clinic occupied two other spaces. The third floor of the building held an art studio for starving artists, under Aunt Sara's sponsorship. The second floor was the dance studio.

"This is wonderful, Letty, but how do you support it? I know nonprofits aren't rolling in money," Ashley asked.

"It's a struggle. In the case of Joy's Center, the small businesses help keep the building open for the dance studio. In my case, the dance studio helps make it possible to keep the building open and provide low-cost rent to the other nonprofits. And it's partly due to you," Letty said as they walked up the staircase to the second-floor dance studio.

"What did I do?"

"You made it into Juilliard. Do you have any idea how hard that is? When word about your success spread through the dance community in Michigan, I started getting calls to take on more students, ones who could afford to pay well for their lessons. Those students helped me provide free tuition for poor students, which was my dream. They are the bread and butter of the studio. But you must remember, I have a much greater population to draw students and patrons from, unlike Cascade Falls. And my connection to Alvin Ailey helped."

Ashley looked about the studio in awe. Several classes were in session, everything from modern dance, to hip hop, and classical ballet.

"I always knew you could do it."

"Doesn't mean it's easy," Letty responded.

"I know," Ashley began, then was joined by all three women in chorus. "Money is always a problem when you run a non-profit."

"What's this about?" Ashley heard a familiar voice ring out at the top of the stairs. Ashley looked up and recognized the woman rushing down the stairs to greet them.

"Aunt Sara." Ashley hugged her. "So good to see you."

"I'm glad we could get together before the wedding. I know it'll be great, but with all the people, there's rarely time for a real conversation. Next time you come to Michigan I want you to stay in Detroit with me part of the time."

They headed out to Letty's favorite deli where they were able to sit outside and enjoy people watching while talking.

"Ashley, tell us about New York and being a prima ballerina. Is it everything you dreamed it would be?" Aunt Sara asked.

"That and more." Ashley picked at her salad. What to tell? So much and yet so little. "I love New York. There's always something going on."

"Not like Cascade Falls," Aunt Sara interjected.

"No, but Cascade Falls isn't meant to be New York. It isn't that bad. It has its own character."

"That coming from the girl who left Cascade Falls for New York, via Detroit, and kicked its dirt from her feet," Aunt Kathleen said.

"What do you want me to say? That New York isn't all it's cracked up to be and Cascade Falls is the best?"

"Just speak your mind—not that that has ever been a problem for you." Aunt Kathleen laughed.

"New York is everything it's cracked up to be and then some. I love New York. But Cascade Falls is everything it is meant to be. I love them both for different reasons."

"Doesn't sound like Ashley will be leaving New York for Cascade Falls or any place else in the near future," Letty said.

"Hey, wait. Is this a set up? Four against one?"

"More like two against two against one," Aunt Sara said. "Letty and I would love to have you move to Detroit, when you're done in New York, that is. And your aunt Kathleen and Chloe would love to have you move back to Cascade Falls. We all four would love to have you back in Michigan."

"So, you all have ulterior motives."

"You could say that, but only if what we want fits with what you want," Aunt Sara said.

"That's according to Sara. As far as I'm concerned, there's no question about what you should do when you are ready to retire," Aunt Kathleen said.

"And if I want to stay in New York?"

"Don't you want to get married and have kids?" Aunt Kathleen asked.

"Who says I can't do that in New York?" It was on her tongue to tell them about Michael, but she couldn't tell them before she told her parents.

"And who says she has to get married?" Letty added. So far Letty had refused that path, but not for lack of options. "You might say, I'm married to Freedom House. All the dancers, all the children who come here, they are my children."

"Okay, okay. Enough of this. Can we talk about something else besides me? I mean, I know I may have given the impression in the past that I only want to talk about myself …"

"No!" All four feigned surprise. "You?"

"Okay, maybe I deserve that. But please …" Ashley took a sip of her sparkling water. "Enough already."

"There is one more thing, if you would allow me," Letty said.

Ashley crossed her arms in front of her on the table, lowered her head onto her arms then raised her eyes in a sign of mock resignation.

"I mean what I said about you helping to make Freedom House a reality. There is something else you could do." When Ashley didn't respond, Letty took that as an affirmation to go on. The other three women nodded at her. "Having a prima ballerina, especially one from Michigan, do a performance at a fundraiser for Freedom House would be a huge financial boast. There are a lot of people in Detroit who would be willing to pay for that, and even more for the opportunity to go to a reception in your honor afterwards."

"And even more money to have dinner with you," Chloe added.

"Wait. You're in on this, too?" Ashley asked Chloe.

"We've all discussed it. It could be a joint fundraiser for Freedom House and Joy's Center. We would get a better turn-out in Detroit. Or we could do two fundraisers, one in Detroit, one in Cascade Falls. What do you think?"

"Is this what you wanted all along?"

"You know how it goes," Letty said. "Door-in-your-face technique. You ask for something big, figuring they will say no, then you ask for a smaller favor figuring they would feel bad about saying no and say yes to the smaller request you really wanted."

"Not that we don't want you to move back to Cascade Falls," Aunt Kathleen added.

Ashley looked at the four women, shook her head and laughed. "I love you. Of course, I'll do it."

"We knew you would," Aunt Sara said.

"I didn't know. After all, we are talking about Ashley." Aunt Kathleen smiled and raised her eyebrows.

"This wasn't just about a fundraiser. We really did want to spend time with you too," Chloe said.

"But if in the process we could do something to help both dance studios …" Aunt Kathleen added.

"Who knows? Maybe I can do better than just one prima ballerina. Maybe I could get other members of The Company to perform with me."

"More than I could ask for," Letty said.

"Not me. I am her favorite aunt after all," Aunt Kathleen said.

"Hey!" Aunt Sara said.

"You know it's true, right Ashley?" Aunt Kathleen gave her another conspiratorial smile.

Once again, she was the center of the conversation. She didn't mind it. Now, how to approach Michael about funding for yet another dance studio?

Chapter 24

Caleb and Olivia were in the backyard when she arrived that evening.

"Olivia helped me prepare dinner. One of her favorites," Caleb told her as she joined them. "Grilled cheese. Though for you I got some fancy cheese, feta, and added spinach to your sandwich. Right, Olivia?" Olivia continued playing with her dolls, ignoring both of them. "I'm afraid I'm not much of a cook, especially for a vegetarian. I can do a mean hamburger or hotdog. There are veggie hotdogs, aren't there?"

"Grilled cheese will be perfect."

"And a salad. I know how to buy those bagged salads, though Olivia and I don't usually eat them."

Ashley smiled. "I'm sure it will be fabulous."

Caleb brought out a tray of gooey grilled sandwiches with cheese dripping out the sides, a salad, and a bowl of watermelon slices, and set it on a picnic table. "I remember how you were always watching your weight in high school. I'm assuming that hasn't changed."

"Actually, it's worse now. The salad and watermelon look delicious."

"And, lemon water, not lemonade."

"Perfect," Ashley said.

Olivia set her dolls aside and joined them at the picnic table. She picked at her food, eating part of her sandwich, ignoring the salad on her plate but asking for more watermelon.

"I see you have a ballerina in training, based on how much she eats," Ashley teased.

"Can we have ice cream, Daddy?"

"Or not," Ashley added.

"Olivia, we aren't done yet."

"I'm done. You said if I was good, we would have ice cream."

"And you will. Why don't you go play while Ashley and I finish?" Olivia ran off to the swing-set and swung on her belly on the swing.

"Progress. She didn't stamp her foot and demand that I leave," Ashley said.

"I think she might almost like you."

"That would be too much to ask." Ashley took another bite of watermelon.

"How was Detroit?" Caleb took a bite of his grilled sandwich, licking cheese off his fingers.

"Fun, though I was ambushed."

"Ambushed? How?"

"All four want me to help fundraise for their dance studios."

Caleb laughed. "Sounds like a set-up all right. And you said yes."

"Of course."

"Does that mean you'll be back sooner rather than later?" Caleb popped the last bite of his sandwich in his mouth.

"It depends on when we can set it up."

Olivia came back to the picnic table. "Are you done yet?"

Ashley looked at Caleb and laughed. "I guess I am now."

They proceeded to get ice cream then went to the park again. Later Caleb put Olivia to bed, then he rejoined Ashley in the backyard, handing her a bottle of water.

"In bed?" Ashley asked as he sat down next to her.

"Yes, reading her books. It's hard to fall asleep when the sun is still out." Caleb took a swig of beer.

"So, are you bringing anyone to the wedding?" Ashley asked.

"You mean a date?"

"Yes, a date."

"Chelsea's coming with us, but it's hardly a date. She's going to help me with Olivia. She's been a lot of support to me since Stacey's death."

"Like Stacey was after your mom's death. Are you sure she sees it that way?"

"Are you hinting at something?"

"I'm just saying, I see a pattern here. Pointing it out in case you hadn't noticed."

"And you're bringing, what's his name? Michael?"

"Yes, Michael." Ashley took a drink of water. "You didn't tell me how Stacey died."

"It's not exactly something I want to relive." Caleb took another swig of beer while Ashley waited. "Stacey loved Lake Michigan. Went there every summer as a child. Once we were married, we camped there every summer, sometimes two or three times a season."

"Lake Michigan is the best."

Caleb ignored the comment. "You should have seen her. Every morning she would get up at dawn and race along the shoreline. Then she would run along the pier to the light house and greet the morning. Sometimes she would do yoga. Sometimes she would sit in quiet meditation. Our first years together I would run with her. Then Olivia came along. I was happy to stay at the campsite, sleep in and take care of Olivia while Stacey ran and worked out. It was her routine. You know she was a dancer?"

"Yes."

"A good one, though not as good as you. No one was as good as you. But that was okay. She always had time for me and Olivia and other aspects of life."

Unlike me. Ashley thought better of saying that. "I think I would have liked her."

"I think you would have. We went every June. That morning there were high wind warnings. I tried to get her to stay at the campsite, but there was no stopping her. She insisted she knew what she was doing.

"When she didn't return by mid-morning, I was worried. It wasn't like Stacey. I put Olivia in her stroller and went to the beach. I asked everyone I saw if they had seen her, but no one had. When I called the Coast Guard, they couldn't tell me anything. They said there had been some reports of people missing but no confirmations. They had search teams out. When I called the police, they told me they couldn't issue a missing person warrant until she had been gone for twenty-four hours." Caleb stared out across the yard as he spoke, but Ashley could tell he was somewhere else, as he related the story.

"I took Olivia back to our campsite, waited, hoped, and prayed. Nothing. No word. Olivia kept asking me where Mommy was. That was a long day. When the Coast Guard showed up that evening, I knew it couldn't be good news. Knew it in my gut. It was in knots." He took another swig of beer before continuing.

"First he told me there had been a report by another jogger that morning about seeing someone blown off the pier by a wave. He hadn't been able to reach the woman in time. He had called the Coast Guard and they had sent out a search team. Then he asked me to come with him to identify a body that had come ashore ten miles down from where Stacey usually ran. I prayed it wasn't her.

"I took Olivia with me but when it came time to identify the body, she stayed with another Coast Guard officer. I couldn't bear to have her see her mother like that."

"It was her."

"Yes. Bloated and pale. Not the Stacey I knew. Just a shell. Her spirit was gone, but it was her." Caleb leaned forward, placing his elbows on his knees as he stared at the horizon.

"All Olivia knew was that her mother went for a run one morning and never came back. No wonder she thinks her mother is coming back. I've had a hard enough time accepting it myself. I kept thinking she would show up alive. Even after I saw her body, I didn't want to believe it."

He looked over at her. "Did you have a hard time believing your mother was dead?"

"No, not that I remember, but my mom was sick for two years before she died. I had plenty of time to see her get weaker and suffer. I don't know which is worse. It must have been terrible for both of you. How did you get through it?"

"I know you may not want to hear this, but God."

She didn't want to hear it. Was he going to go all Jesus freak on her? Witness to her?

"My senior year was hard. I kept up appearances, played basketball, went to work, but I struggled. You were gone. My mom was sick off and on and my dad … Well, you know we didn't get along." He shrugged before continuing.

"I knew you didn't believe in God. I wanted to decide for myself. Did I or didn't I believe? I tried reading different theories, even read Stephen Hawking's theory about the spontaneous eruption of the universe. Didn't really understand it."

"He's a genius. Many don't understand him."

"I may not be a genius, but I don't see why God couldn't have been part of that spontaneous eruption, or Big Bang. Didn't prove that God didn't exist to me." When Ashley didn't respond, he kept talking.

"When I told myself I didn't believe, it seemed the darkness I was experiencing became darker. When I tried out belief, it lifted. Not entirely, not right away, but gradually, over time. Things got better. I found ways to cope until I was able to move out. Then I went to college."

"Did it occur to you that maybe it got better not because of God, but the passage of time?"

"It did occur to me, but no. It was more than that. I figured I couldn't prove whether God existed. Smarter people than me had tried and failed, but I made a choice for God and never looked back. My life got better after that. I don't know what I would have done when Stacey died if not for God. I don't know how to explain it. It's just a feeling, a presence. It didn't take away the pain. It just helped me carry it."

"If it helps you, then I'm glad for you."

Caleb stared across the backyard to the sky. Scallops of pink spread across the darkening sky as the sun started its slide behind the horizon.

"They say you never forget your first love." Caleb continued to stare at the sky, not looking at her as he spoke. "I've never forgotten you, Ashley. That doesn't mean I didn't love Stacey. I did with all my heart." Caleb took a swig of beer, still focusing on the horizon. "You were two different people. I love you both but in different ways, for different reasons."

Ashley stared at the sky then reached for Caleb's beer, took a sip then handed it back before responding. "When my dad started dating Ava, I was angry. I thought it meant he didn't love my mom anymore. But now I know it's possible to have more than one great love in your life."

"You never get over the loss of a loved one. You have to keep going. Somehow you get through. Was that how it was for you?"

Was that how it was? Ashley watched the light pinks darken to a red hue as the sun disappeared.

"I don't know. Do you ever get over the loss of your mother? Sometimes I think I have, then something happens to remind me again of what I lost. The grief does lessen over time. It morphs, changes shape. Sometimes it catches me off guard, like when Olivia told me about her mother. But it lessens."

Ashley continued to watch the sunset. Rich, deep hues of pink and red, spreading out along the horizon. Had God created this display for her? But wait, she didn't believe in God. It was just an act of nature.

"I never forgot you either, Caleb. I guess I never entirely stopped loving you. I still have your class ring. I keep it in my jewelry box." That doesn't mean I don't love Michael, she added to herself.

"I'm glad you have the ring. I meant for you to have it, or I wouldn't have given it to you."

Ashley turned her face from the sunset and realized Caleb was staring at her.

"I never got over you, Ashley. Not entirely. There's always been a part of me thinking, wondering, when you would come back." Caleb leaned in. This time he was able to softly place a kiss on her lips before a little voice rang out.

"Daddy!" Olivia was at her bedroom window.

"I guess that's my cue to leave." Ashley started to lean back away from him.

"Don't. Don't leave, not yet." He turned her face back towards his and kissed her again. This time their lips pressed firmly against each other as Ashley responded, kissing him back, then gasped. What was she doing? What about Michael? She pulled back.

"Daddy!" Olivia shouted again.

"Now I have to go." Ashley slipped away to her car before he could call her back, before she could give into the almost overpowering desire to kiss him again and again.

"Coming," she heard Caleb call as she drove away, his kiss burning on her lips.

Chapter 25

Ashley called Michael as soon as she got home. She needed to reassure herself, remind herself of her life in New York. When he didn't answer she texted him, "Called to say I love you and miss you," with heart emojis.

Ashley tossed and turned most of the night. What had she been thinking? Why hadn't she told Caleb about her engagement? Caleb could be trusted to keep it secret from her family until she was ready to tell them. She knew that. Ava was right. Sometimes a secret takes on a life of its own. You can't share it no matter how much you may want to.

And what was all that God talk? She expected it from Uncle Joe, him being a pastor and all, but Ava and now Caleb? Who was Ava to say she would pray for her? What does prayer have to do with anything? She either had cancer or she didn't. No amount of prayer would change that physical reality. She would know when the doctor's office called with results. When would that be?

And Caleb. Maybe believing in God worked for him. It helped him feel better. It was all about gut feelings, not knowledge. She had thought better of him. She didn't need a crutch to get through this life. She was doing fine on her own, thank you. Look at all she had achieved through her own pluck and determination. No wonder she had stayed away for so many years. How much longer could she take all this God talk? Prayers at every meal. And it was going to get worse. There will be prayers at the wedding, prayers at the rehearsal and rehearsal dinner, prayers at the reception. Why couldn't Jacob and Josie have had a nice pantheistic service — or whatever it was they believed — in the redwoods? That would have been more tolerable. How was she going to survive this?

Ashley was up and ready to go by nine that morning. There was a text from Michael. "Sorry I missed your call. Business-related social event. Will call tonight!" She would have to wait until then to vent her frustration.

"Have to make up for my missed workouts," Ashley told her dad and Ava as she left for the dance studio. Jacob was just getting up as she rushed out the door.

This time the studio was silent when she unlocked the door. Good. Even Aunt Kathleen and Chloe weren't there yet. She didn't want to see anyone.

She stopped at the picture of her mother that hung in the hallway between classrooms and offices. Still there. Why hadn't she noticed it before? Maybe all the noise and commotion from the dance camp. There was her mother, around her age, pregnant with Grace. By the time she was Ashley's current age, her mother had already had two children, with another on the way. That was the same year she'd been diagnosed with breast cancer. She had refused her doctor's recommendation that she abort the baby and aggressively treat her cancer. That was why Ashley blamed Grace for her death.

At least Ashley didn't have that to worry about. No baby for her.

Her mother was in her dance clothes and pointe shoes, posed on a high wire amid the clouds. The same pink she had seen last night marked the angels in the clouds against the blue sun-lit sky. Her mother's arms were raised in praise.

How had her mother maintained her balance that year? How had she done it? Running a dance studio, raising kids? Ashley had a greater appreciation for her mother. All Ashley had to do was maintain her position as prima amid the politics of the dance company. That seemed like nothing compared to what her mother had dealt with.

She knew her mother was a woman of faith. What would she think about her daughter, the prima ballerina? Would she be proud of her? Would her mother be upset about her lack of faith?

Ashley jumped at the sound of a door opening. "Aunt Kathleen. I didn't know you were going to be in today."

"There's more work to running an arts center than being here for dance camp."

Ashley didn't respond at first. "I was looking at my mother's picture. I wonder what she would think about me being a prima ballerina."

"She would have been so proud of you. But then she would have been proud of you no matter what you did, as long as you were happy and following your dream. You are happy, aren't you, Ashley?"

"Yes, I am. But sometimes I wonder. What happens when you achieve everything you ever dreamed of? I mean, what next?"

"I guess you find new dreams. But what do I know? I never achieved anything like you three kids. I know your mom would be proud of all three of you. I am too. And not because you're a prima ballerina. Because you are my audacious niece, my talented spunky niece who never let anything or anyone keep her from achieving her dreams."

For some reason that didn't feel like a compliment. "When you say it that way, it seems awful. I mean everyone keeps telling me how focused I was. But was I heartless, Aunt Kathleen? Was I so driven that I didn't care about anyone or anything but myself and dance?" Ashley fought back tears as she spoke.

"But if that's what it takes to make it in this business? It would be applauded in a man."

"Would it? I wonder." Ashley studied her mother's picture.

Aunt Kathleen stepped up next to her. "You know, Ashley, what I said about your mother wanting you to come back and keep the dance studio going. It's not true. I'm the one who wants that. I thought a little guilt might be a good thing."

"I know. That's what Dad and Jacob said."

"What did they say?"

"That you would do anything to keep the studio and center going, and to get me to move back here."

"They're right." Aunt Kathleen gazed at the picture too. "Your mom would want you to be happy. That was just how she was."

Ashley sighed. "I wish I remembered her better. Sometimes it feels like she has slipped away from me. How much did I know her? I was just a kid. I only knew her as a child knows. I wish I could have known her better."

"Any time you want me to tell you about your mother, what I remember, just say so. And I'm sure Sara would be happy to share memories of her sister." Aunt Kathleen wrapped her arm around Ashley as they stood in silence and looked at the picture together.

"That would be nice. I'd appreciate that." Ashley sighed again then turned away from the picture. "Right now, though, it's time for me to get to work."

"Me too. Meet me for lunch?"

"Sure. We can talk more about my mom then."

Ashley went into Studio One, stretched her legs, did her warmup routine, then turned on her I-pod for music. She remembered her mom dancing between classes, stretching then turning on her favorite music. Sometimes her mom was working on choreography for an upcoming recital. Sometimes she danced for the joy of it. Other times her mother wept. Ashley wondered if her mother realized she had been watching her, not all the time, but enough.

Ashley remembered entering the room once when she must have been Olivia's age. Her mother was crying. Ashley didn't know why.

"Don't cry, Mommy. I'm here."

"Ashley." Her mother wiped away the tears and smiled. "It's okay to cry. You know that, don't you? Sometimes life is hard and you feel like crying. It doesn't always mean anything is wrong. It could mean something is right. I'm sad, but my heart is filled with so much love. For you, your dad, Jacob, and Grace. I'm so blessed to have you in my life. Never forget that."

How had she forgotten? She remembered how she had blamed Grace at first for her mom being sick. And how she had blamed God. That was back when she believed in God.

When she had first told her dad and Ava she didn't believe in God, they had wanted her to talk to Uncle Joe, since he was a pastor. They thought she didn't believe in God because of what had happened to her mom. They were wrong. To blame God, you had to believe in God. She didn't blame God, nor did she believe in God. Sometimes things happen. People die. God has nothing to do with it.

Talking to Uncle Joe had been okay, but he hadn't changed her mind. What he did do though was to get everyone else off her back, telling them about free will. God gave us free will so we could choose to believe, choose to love God. She hadn't believed in that either, but her parents had lightened up on her, so she appreciated Uncle Joe talking to them.

Ashley knew Uncle Joe figured eventually she would come around to believe in God if they left her alone. He was wrong. It wasn't a childish stage she would grow out of. She didn't believe in God or spirits. When we die, we die. Our bodies go back into the earth where we return to dust.

And yet, here in the dance studio, in the classroom where her mother had spent so much of her sweat and tears, she almost felt her spirit.

Chapter 26

Ashley looked at her phone. Caleb. What was this about? She had just gotten home from teaching Chloe's advanced class.

"Ashley, I have a huge favor to ask. I'm going to be stuck at work until six and Olivia needs to be picked up at day care by five at the latest. Chelsea isn't available. Could you pick her up for me?"

"I'm supposed to be going to Grace's for dinner. I was just getting ready to go."

"Perfect. You can take Olivia with you. She'd love it. You can pick her up any time you want as long as it's by five. I wouldn't ask you if I had anyone else."

Ashley hesitated. It was only three. What would she do with a five-year-old for three hours?

"Sure. I can do it." What would it hurt? If there were problems, Grace could help her out.

"Thanks, Ashley. You're a life-saver."

No one had called her that before. But then she was going to be helping the arts center and Freedom House with fundraising. This helping-others thing was new. She wasn't sure whether she liked it.

Ashley arrived at the day care center a little before four. Kids were outside in the play area, running and climbing on play structures. She waved at Olivia. Olivia looked at her and ran in the opposite direction.

She went into the office and told the receptionist she was there to pick up Olivia Marshall.

"You must be Ms. Reese. Olivia's father told us you'd be picking her up. I need to see some ID."

Ashley pulled out her driver's license.

"Hmmm. New York."

What was it about New York driver's license? "That's not a problem, is it?"

The woman looked at her picture on the ID then at her. "Not for me. You're the one who has to live there." She handed the license back. "I'll get Olivia."

Olivia frowned when she saw Ashley.

"Olivia, this nice lady is going to take you home," the receptionist said.

"I don't want to go with her."

Ashley squatted down in front of her. "Olivia, your daddy can't come right now. We can get ice cream."

"No. I don't want to go with you."

Ashley tried to take her hand. Olivia refused.

"Is there a problem?" the receptionist asked.

"No, not at all. Just a minute." She stepped aside and called Caleb.

"Hey Ashley, what's wrong?"

"We have a problem. Olivia refuses to go with me."

"Just tell her I can't come right now."

"I did. I can't drag her kicking and screaming out of the day care center. People have been arrested for less."

"Okay. Put her on the phone."

Ashley handed Olivia her phone. "Your dad wants to talk to you."

"Yes, Daddy… I don't want to… okay, Daddy," Ashley heard on her side of the phone. What Caleb was saying she didn't know, but it appeared to be working. Olivia handed her the phone.

"I don't know what you said, but it seems to have worked."

"I told her you were going to take her to a farm with horses." Now why hadn't she thought of that? "And I promised her ice cream on the way home."

"Okay, Olivia. Are you ready to go?" Ashley held out her hand. Olivia allowed Ashley to take her hand, eyeing her the whole way out to the parking lot. Ashley strapped her into the back seat of her car.

"You like horses?" Ashley tried to engage Olivia in a conversation.

"Do you like my dad?" Ashley could see Olivia glaring at her through the rearview mirror.

"Your dad and I are friends from way back."

"I saw him kiss you. I don't like you. When are you going to leave so my mom can come back?"

Ashley pulled off the road into a parking lot then turned around so she could look at Olivia. What could she say that wouldn't cause the girl to jump out of the car or start screaming?

"You love your mother very much."

"Yes."

"No one can ever take your mother's place. You know that, don't you? I would never try to take your mother's place." Olivia didn't respond. "You know, when I was your age, my mother went away and never came back. She died. I was very sad for a long time. I wanted my mother to come back, but she had been very sick for a long time. I didn't want her to be sick anymore."

"My mother wasn't sick. She went away, but she's coming back. She wouldn't have left without saying goodbye."

"I'm sure she didn't mean to leave without saying goodbye."

"My grandma says she's with Jesus. Jesus doesn't need my mother. I think Jesus is mean to keep my mother from me."

Now would be a good time for Uncle Joe to show up, but of course he wasn't there. All she had was herself. "Olivia, do you remember the big picture at the dance studio, the one of the woman dancing on a wire?"

"Yes."

"That's my mother. She's up in heaven now, dancing in the clouds." So, it was a lie, a white lie. White lies didn't hurt, her grandma used to say. And they could help. "Do you think your mother is in the clouds dancing with my mom?"

"But I want her here."

"I wish my mother were here too, but when I'm sad, I think about her dancing in heaven. Then I feel better."

"But my mother never said goodbye."

"If your mother was here, what do you think she would say?"

"I don't know."

"I think she would tell you how much she loved you and that she was sorry to leave you. Then she would kiss you, tell you to kiss your daddy for her and would say goodbye."

"But will she be coming back?"

"No, Olivia, she won't be coming back, but she will be in your heart." She remembered all the times people had told her that about her mom. She hadn't liked it back then, didn't like it any more now but she didn't know what else to say. Streams of tears slid down the girl's face as she sucked on her fingers. Ashley climbed out of the car and slid into the back seat where she could hug the girl, her own tears mixing with Olivia's. Would she always feel this pain where her mother was concerned? But somehow, sharing this with Olivia, it felt lighter.

When Olivia seemed ready, Ashley asked, "Do you want to go see the horses?"

"Yeth," Olivia said through her fingers. Ashley wiped Olivia's tear-stained face before going into the driver's seat and pulling back onto the road. Surreptitiously, she wiped her own as well, glancing back at the little girl.

Grace came out on the porch as Ashley's car pulled up the farm's driveway.

"I'm sorry I'm late," Ashley said as she rounded her car and opened the rear door. "I brought an extra guest." Olivia unbuckled herself and climbed out of the car. "But don't worry. She won't eat much unless, of course, you're having ice cream."

"Hi, Olivia," Grace said. "I'm glad you could join us. Do you want to see the horses?"

Olivia nodded.

When Grace took her hand, Olivia looked at Ashley. "You're coming too?" She reached for Ashley's hand.

"Of course." Ashley accepted the small grasp then looked over Olivia's head at Grace and smiled.

"It seems someone has made a friend," Grace said.

The threesome paused at the top of the hill. As Ashley looked across the pasture to where the horses were grazing, Olivia broke loose from their hands and ran down the hill to the fence.

Ashley glanced at Grace, shrugged and took off running after her. By the time they reached the fence, Olivia was laughing and giggling. Ashley laughed too in response. Funny how just a short time ago they had both been in tears. Ashley tickled Olivia then picked her up and placed her feet on a fence rail so could see over the top.

"Do you want to feed them?" Grace asked when she reached them. She made a clicking sound, then called to the horses. They raised their heads and approached the fence, the younger ones running ahead of the older mares.

"Whoa," Olivia said and reached for Ashley when they got closer. Ashley picked Olivia up and held her so she could see the horses yet maintain a comfortable distance.

"This one is Eleanor, or Lady Eleanor of Aquitaine." Grace's voice rose appropriately to signify the horse's stature. Olivia giggled. "And her babies, Isabella, or Izzy, and Montebello, or Monty."

"Your babies," Ashley corrected her.

"And this one," Grace reached through the fence and rubbed the mare's nose. "This one is Lady Mercedes, or Lady. She's going to have a baby this summer."

"I thought you had decided not to breed them anymore. What made you change your mind?"

"We had, at least for Eleanor. One twin pregnancy is enough for any older mare. But then, we figured Lady had one more pregnancy in her. She's doing well. Just look at her."

The mare's coat was silky smooth. She was the picture of health. Olivia reached tentatively over the fence and touched the mare's back.

"And this raucous boy is Sir Perceval, or Percy, or Peanut." Grace bent down and pulled some long grass. "Would you like to feed Peanut?"

Olivia took the grass and carefully laid it across the fence rail, while clinging to Ashley. Peanut took the grass, smacking his lips as he did. Olivia dropped the grass when he got too close but laughed as the colt finished it off.

"Here, you can feed the horses from behind the fence." Ashley put Olivia down, pulled out another handful of grass and showed Olivia how to put it between the fence rails for the horses. Olivia jumped each time one came near but giggled in response. While she was busy with the horses, Ashley looked over at her sister.

"You know the picture of Mom at the dance studio?"

"Of course. My first baby picture, in utero."

"I was looking at it today." Ashley gazed across the field. "I remembered how I blamed you for Mom's cancer. I never said I was sorry for that, did I?"

"No, you didn't, but that's okay."

"No, it's not. I am sorry. It was wrong of me."

"You were just a kid. Olivia's age. You never said anything I didn't think myself most of my life."

"I'm sorry, Grace. So sorry. Kids can be mean."

"Yes, they can. I appreciate you saying so, but I'm okay." She smiled and looked at Ashley. "I guess we all carry our own scars from Mom's death. At some point, you get over and get on."

"Is that what you've done?"

"You remember how I had emergency heart surgery last spring?"

"Yes. I'm sorry I wasn't able to come."

"No need to be. I got the flowers." Ashley grimaced while Grace laughed. "No, I mean it. The surgery did more than repair my physical heart. It repaired the hole in my heart." Grace looked tentatively at Ashley before proceeding. "While I was under, I saw Mom. It was real. When I woke up, it hurt physically, but I felt at peace, an amazing peace."

"Drugs will do that."

"No, it was more than drugs. It was real, as real as you standing by me right now."

Ashley fidgeted. She wanted to put her hands over her ears and stomp her foot, like Olivia, but restrained herself. She knew it was childish but…

"I'm glad that worked for you."

"And now, I've never felt better. I never realized—all those times when I couldn't seem to keep up—there was something wrong. I just thought that was how it was."

"Hey. I'm sorry if I ever made fun of you for not being able to keep up with me and Jacob."

"You were just being a big sister." Josie appeared on the deck, calling to them. Grace waved at her then let out a sigh. "If only it were that easy for Josie. If only there was a single surgery that would take care of all of her problems." Grace smiled. "I think that means it's time to eat." She looked at Olivia. "Someday Olivia, when you're older, you can ride the horses. Would you like that?"

"Yes, Aunt Grace."

"It seems you've been elevated to aunt status," Ashley said. "And what about me?"

"You're just Ashley."

Both women laughed at this.

"Olivia, race me to the top?" Ashley asked. "Ready, set, go."

Olivia took off, her little legs struggling to make it up the incline, while Ashley and Grace took their time sauntering up the hill. Ashley extended a helping hand of support whenever Grace faltered from the additional weight she was carrying.

A figure appeared at the top of the hill. Caleb.

"Daddy." Olivia ran toward him. He picked her up and waited for the two women.

"Thank you so much." Caleb put Olivia down. "You have no idea how much this means to me. This single parent job, it's hard."

"Any time you need help with Olivia, let us know," Grace told him. "Our baby is going to need a big sister to tease him or her." Grace looked at Olivia and smiled then turned back to Caleb. "You're staying for dinner, aren't you?"

"I've imposed enough."

"Nonsense. Abel doesn't know how to cook anything but double what he needs. He likes to do things in a big way. There's plenty for everyone."

Caleb and Olivia sat down at the table next to Ashley. Jacob and Josie, Grace and Abel, and Abel's grandfather, Lamar, filled the rest of the seats. Without her parents there, Ashley thought they were going to avoid the daily ritual of saying prayers when a small voice sitting beside her, said, "What about grace?"

"Grace is right there," Ashley said.

"No, we always say grace before meals," Olivia stated.

"Grace," Jacob said, just like he had so many times when they had been kids, making fun of Grace's name.

"Ha ha, Jacob. It wasn't funny then and it's still not funny," Grace said. "Olivia, would you like to pray for us?"

"No, Daddy." She tugged on his sleeve.

"How about it, Caleb?" Abel asked.

Caleb took Olivia's hand and Grace's hand. Everyone held hands. Ashley looked around the group, realizing they had all bowed their heads. She looked down sideways at Olivia. She looked almost angelic with her head bowed and eyes closed.

"Lord, we thank you for this gathering of friends and family. We thank you for bringing us safely together and pray for the continued health and safety of all. Bless us, bless our time together, bless our food. Amen."

"Grace," Jacob added.

"Grace," everyone repeated and laughed.

"Amen and pass the food," Lamar said.

"For a minute there I thought you were going to take as long as Uncle Joe, right Ashley?" Jacob said as he reached for the heaping bowl of mashed potatoes.

"You did just fine, Caleb," Grace told him. "Thank you for blessing our table."

Just like Grace, Ashley thought. How had she not recognized how kind and thoughtful her sister had always been?

Caleb insisted on cleaning up after dinner. "It's the least I can do."

"Don't you have to get Olivia home and in bed?" Ashley asked.

"What's another half hour? You can help me."

Olivia was occupied, playing with Jacob and Josie.

"Okay." Ashley went into the kitchen and started rinsing off dishes to put in the dishwasher. "I never did understand why Ava always insisted we rinse the dishes before putting them in the dishwasher. Why even bother with the dishwasher if you wash them before you put them in?"

"Because, if you don't loosen all the crud on the plates, they will be harder to get off after they've run through the dishwasher."

"Sounds like you were brought up in the same school of cleaning."

"No, but Stacey was." Caleb joined her at the sink, dumping scraps of food into the compost container on the counter. "Ashley, about last night ..."

Ashley squirmed. Should she tell him about her engagement to Michael now? But what if someone overheard? "That's okay. It just happened."

"I don't want to give you the wrong impression. I ... I'm ... I'm still getting over Stacey's death, and there's Olivia to consider."

"No, I completely understand."

"I had no right to kiss you like that. I never should have done it. You have your life in New York and I have my life here." Caleb busied himself with rinsing out the sink, avoiding her eyes.

"Right." Ashley avoided him as well.

"So, we're good? No harm, no foul?"

"No, we're good." Ashley focused on the dishes. There. Problem solved. She didn't have to say anything about Michael. Why didn't she feel good about it?

"That's good, because I want us to be friends." Caleb turned to look at her, then turned back away.

Friends. Right.

Caleb called to Olivia after they finished. "Time to go home."

"I don't want to."

Jacob had her on his shoulders. He lowered her down. "You heard your dad. It's time to go home. You can come over again."

Olivia took Ashley's hand. "I want Ashley to put me to bed."

"But Olivia, Ashley came in her own car. She isn't coming home with us."

Olivia continued to hold Ashley's hand.

"How about I put you in your dad's car?" Ashley suggested.

She walked Olivia to the car, buckled her into her car seat and gave her a kiss on the cheek. "You be good for your daddy. You know he loves you very much."

Caleb was waiting when Ashley shut the door. "I don't know what you did? How did she go from refusing to go with you, to not wanting you to leave?"

"Just girl talk, not something you would understand."

"Well, if you would be willing to try, I'd be willing to listen."

Ashley smiled and waved at Olivia through the window while Caleb climbed in the driver's seat.

Girl talk. Ashley stood on the porch and watched as they drove away.

Chapter 27

One more day till all the festivities began. One more day till Michael arrived. She had filled Michael in on Freedom House when she had talked to him the previous night.

"I've already talked to Grandpa about helping with Joy's Studio of Dance. What's one more?"

She knew she could count on him. How did she deserve him? Would she know the results of the biopsy by the time he arrived?

"Any word?" Ava asked after her dad left for the day.

"No, but you'll be the first person I tell when I hear. You'll be the only person I tell." She hadn't even told Audra. There was something about being here, in Cascade Falls. She didn't know what it was. She just knew she couldn't tell Audra, the one person she shared everything with. Audra had known about Michael before their first date. Ashley called whenever she had a minute to spare. Audra prattled on, filling her in on what was happening in New York, the latest Company gossip. But Ashley had not told Audra about the possibility of having breast cancer. Telling someone would have made it more real. How could it be more real than it already was?

Ashley picked up her dance bag and headed out the door. She needed another good workout.

"Don't forget. You have to try on and pick up your dress today. Three o'clock."

"I'll be there." After that, no more big meals or over-indulging in alcohol or sweets. Not that she had done that this week. What with the limited vegetarian options, she easily made up for her indulgences over the weekend ... in time to indulge more this weekend. Then back to New York and her real life. By then she would know her fate. Either the scare over breast cancer would be just a blip in her otherwise fabulous life, or it would become a reality that would change her future.

This time she didn't linger in front of her mom's picture. She headed into Studio One. Maybe Grace had had a psychedelic experience of their mom while under drugs. That was Grace, not her. She didn't need any ghost of her mother telling her how much she loved her. Ashley knew how much her mom had loved her while on this earth. Now she was gone, and so was the love.

"I was told I would find you here." Grandma. She quietly let herself into the studio.

"Hi, Grandma. Why are you here?"

"You. That's why. I thought maybe we could do lunch, just the two of us, before the onslaught. I can't believe you've been here ten days already and I've hardly seen you."

"Sorry, Grandma."

"You'll make it up to me by having lunch today."

"As soon as I'm done."

"I'll wait. You don't mind if I watch? I'll sit quietly in the corner."

"No, Grandma. Go ahead."

It took more than one eighty-year-old grandmother to distract her from her routine. The sense of her mother's presence was less today, as was expected. Everything was back on target for her. Only four more days till she was back home. No more former boyfriends to confuse her, or little girls to tug at her heart. Now, if only she had the results from the biopsy ...

She was breathing hard by the end of her workout. A slight ripple of applause sounded from the corner of the room.

"Bravo."

Ashley curtseyed as her grandmother approached, tears in her eyes.

"You remind me so much of your mother. She would have been so proud of you."

"You think so?"

"I know so. Now go get changed so this grandmother can show off her famous granddaughter."

If Ashley had been worried about another set-up, she should have known better. This was Grandma, not Aunt Kathleen. Ashley loved them both, as different as they were. Aunt Kathleen was more like her, driven to succeed. But Grandma … she was everything a grandma was supposed to be, though not plump and squishy like fairy-tale grandmothers. Still there was plenty of love in that frame.

They ordered quickly. "I can't believe it's been ten years since you were last home. Where did the years go?" her grandmother said.

"Grandma, I keep telling you to come to New York."

"I know. We talked about it, Peter and I. Don't know why we never made it. Something always came up. And here it is, ten years later, and we still haven't seen you dance in New York."

"Don't let another ten years pass without coming. If you can't get Peter to come, you and Aunt Kathleen can come. Make it a girls' weekend."

"I will. Now tell me about you. Is there anyone special in your life?"

"Why does everyone keep asking me that? Why isn't it okay for a woman to put her career first?"

"Ashley, you know I'd be the last person to suggest that. I've always been proud of your success."

"Sorry, Grandma. Just touchy, I guess. I am seeing someone. Michael. You'll meet him tomorrow. Now can we talk about something else?"

"Okay. You tell me. What would you like to talk about?"

"How about how you always made the holidays so special and how we went to the apple orchard every fall. Or what it was like growing up in Cascade Falls, or what my dad was like as a kid."

"That's a tall order. I don't know where to begin."

"Or my mom. What can you tell me about my mom?"

"Your mom?" Grandma's face softened into a smile. "Your mom was always at our house—that is, when she wasn't dancing.

Your mom and dad were friends in high school, until your dad finally realized there was something more there."

"Men." Ashley shook her head. "They can be so dense."

"They can be slow at times. Your dad was a good kid."

"Unlike Aunt Kathleen."

"That's another story. They both had their challenges, what with their dad, your grandfather, dying when they were so young. For some reason, Kathleen took it harder. Or maybe your dad just didn't show it as much."

"I remember Great Grandpa, your dad. He was always around, wasn't he? When Dad was growing up."

"Yes. He was a big help."

"Like you and Aunt Kathleen were around when we were little."

"That's right." Grandma paused and looked across the room. "So many good people, come and gone. Your grandfather, great grandfather, your mother. If I didn't have faith, I don't know how I would have managed."

Ashley flinched at the mention of faith. Not Grandma, too. "Grandma, what about my mother?"

Her grandmother returned from where she had gone—that place where she stored her memories. "Your dad was lost when she joined Ballet Magnificat, though he never would admit it. And then she came back, and they were inseparable, until …"

"I know. Until she died."

"That was so long ago. And yet, sometimes it's like it was yesterday. When I watched you dance this morning, it was like watching your mother all over again. For a moment, I thought it was her." Grandma stared past Ashley, a wistful look on her face. Ashley reached across the table for her grandma's hand and squeezed it. Grandma wiped away a tear then smiled. "Funny things happen when you get old. It's like you lose your sense of time. One day runs into another and the past seems more real than the present. And the future …"

"Not you, Grandmother. You're not old."

"Sweet of you to say so, but that doesn't make it true." Grandma pulled a folder out of the bag she was carrying. "I've been waiting for the right time to give you this."

"What is it?"

"It's a collection of poems your mother put together. She gave them to me before she died. Told me to keep them for you, for when you were older."

"You're only giving them to me now?"

"You weren't exactly around, were you? Besides, your mom said to wait till you were her age."

Ashley opened the folder. There were cards from friends, a few pictures, but mostly it was poems hand-written by her mom on notebook paper. There were some on determination, others on being kind. Some classics like *The Road Not Taken*, others she didn't recognize.

"She told me the poems gave her strength, said you would need that strength."

"How did she know that?"

"Who doesn't need strength? Besides, you were the artistic one. That's why she wanted you to have them."

Ashley continued to rifle through the pages until she reached a series of sketches. "I didn't know my mom drew."

"There's a lot you don't know about your mother. How much do any of us know about our mothers when we are children? You had so little time with your mom. She died too soon. Perhaps that's why she wanted you to have these. A chance to get to know her better."

Ashley paused as she reflected on Grandma's words. Was her mother reaching out to her from beyond the grave? Was it possible? She shook her head. "So, Aunt Sara isn't the only one with artistic ability."

"It can run in families—creativity, that is. Dance is just one form of creative expression."

Ashley shut the folder, putting it aside for later when she had time. "Thank you, Grandma. This means so much."

Her grandmother smiled and picked up the menu. "Can I interest you in dessert? Maybe apple pie?"

"The only apple pie worth the calories is yours." Ashley reached across the table and squeezed her grandma's hand. How could she have gone so long without her grandmother's apple pie?

Chapter 28

Ashley met Josie and the other bridesmaids at the dress shop. A quick, last-minute check to make sure all the dresses fit right, then home with the dress in hand. Still no message from the doctor's office. Ashley called and left a message. No news may be good news, or not.

That night it was just her and her parents at dinner. Jacob and Josie were having dinner with Josie's parents. Grace and Abel were home, relaxing before hosting the rehearsal dinner tomorrow. It was nice to be just the three of them.

"I expect this will be our last quiet meal together before the onslaught of people. And then you'll be heading back to New York," her dad said during dinner. "What time is your flight?"

"Three o'clock. That means I have to leave by noon to get to the airport in time."

"You sure you can't stay one more day?" Ava asked.

"You sure you want me that long? I mean, fish and guests start to stink after three days."

"But you're not a guest. You're family. There's always room for family."

"I'm glad you're still saying that after ten days."

"And why wouldn't we?" her dad asked.

That's right. Why wouldn't they? What's not to love?

"Tell us about Michael. What does he do? When do we get to meet him?" her dad asked.

"He's coming tomorrow. May not get here until six or seven, depending on his flight and traffic."

"Is he staying here? It's too hot to put a cot in the attic, but we can work it out. Maybe Jacob could stay at Grace's," her dad surmised.

"He has a room booked. He'll probably have work to do. That's why he didn't want to put anyone out by putting him up."

Her dad shrugged and continued eating. Ava looked over at Ashley. They had already had this conversation. Ava, always one to plan ahead, had asked about Michael on day one. Now would be a good time to tell them …

"Caleb tells me you and Olivia are friends now," her dad changed the subject.

"She's a sweet girl."

"Sad, about her mother. Caleb has it rough."

"No rougher than you when Mom died." She looked at her father, remembering that year before her mom died, how her dad had taken care of her mom. Then the year after her death. Sometimes it had seemed like she had lost both of them, her dad had been so sad. That was before Ava came along.

"I had more family support. Caleb only has Stacey's sister."

"What about her parents?"

"I don't know the whole story but they're not around much. Winter in Florida, travelling, that sort of thing. They don't seem that interested in their granddaughter. I don't think they wanted Stacey to marry Caleb. Said he wasn't good enough."

"Caleb? Not good enough? How could anyone say that?" Ashley shook her head in disbelief.

"Well, he wasn't exactly making a lot of money at the time. I think they wanted Stacey to marry a doctor or lawyer or such. And then, Caleb's father … well, you know his father, though they seem to have patched things up. Still, he's not one for taking care of a small child. Not everyone is blessed with hands-on grandparents like you were."

"How could anyone not love that little girl?" Ava added.

"That's why we try to help Caleb out as much as possible. I know how hard it is to lose a wife, but to lose her the way he did …" He trailed off and shook his head. "Caleb has a strong faith."

Ava nodded in agreement.

"Seeing Olivia reminds me of how I was after Mom died. How awful I behaved, especially to you, Ava."

"You were just a child," her dad said.

"A child who had lost her mother," Ava added.

"Hey, I'm trying to apologize here. Not something I'm exactly used to doing." Ashley blushed and looked down at the table.

"Apology accepted," Ava said.

"How can you be so good to me? The way I've behaved all my life. And then, not coming home for so many years. I'm surprised I'm even welcome. Not only do you welcome me, but you're also ready to welcome Michael, a complete stranger, to stay under your roof."

"He's your friend. Of course, he's welcome," Ava said.

"What else would we do? We're your parents. No matter what you do, or did, we love you," her dad added.

"Even when I act unlovable?"

"Dear, when did you do that?" Ava asked. "No matter how bristly you behaved, we loved the little girl under the nettles. No matter how you tried to push us away, we were always here for you, and still are. We'll be here for you, today, tomorrow and the next day."

Why did Ashley find it so hard to believe this? Maybe this was her opening. Was now the time to tell her dad about the biopsy, and both about Michael? "Dad, Ava …"

Voices sounded at the front door, followed by Aunt Kathleen, Uncle Joe and her cousins, Josh and Stephanie.

"We let ourselves in." Aunt Kathleen led the procession. "We brought dessert!" She held up a box from a local bakery. "Ice cream cake."

"Sorry about barging in like this, but we were talking. Josh and Stephanie mentioned how much they would like to see Ashley, so we said, 'why not?'" Uncle Joe said.

"Of course, we aren't barging in. We're family," Aunt Kathleen said.

"You're always welcome." Ava jumped up and brought dessert plates.

"Especially when you bring dessert," her dad added.

"See, I told you." Aunt Kathleen sat down.

"Where's Gus?" Ava cut the cake into thick pieces. "Not like your grandson to miss out on ice cream cake."

"He's got better things to do than hang out with family," Stephanie said. "He's with his friends."

"That will change when he's older. Right?" Aunt Kathleen directed this at Josh and Stephanie.

"Yeah, it doesn't suck half as much as it used to," Stephanie said.

Ashley passed on the cake. The moment was lost, never to come again. Just as well.

After dinner, Ashley retreated to the deck with Josh and Stephanie. "What's up with you two? No marriage?"

"We could ask the same thing of you," Stephanie said.

"True." Ashley shrugged. "I always thought eventually the two of you would wind up together."

"What? Us?" Josh and Stephanie both laughed.

"Go ahead and laugh. Maybe that's why neither of you have found the right one." Ashley ignored their laughter. "It's not like you're actually brother and sister. You didn't even live together as a family." By the time Aunt Kathleen and Uncle Joe had married, they had both been in college.

"Yeah, but there's still the yuck factor," Stephanie said.

"What's so yucky?" Josh asked. "You didn't think I was yucky when you kissed me in high school."

"That was before I got to know the real you." At one time Stephanie had had a crush on Josh. Even Ashley had known about it.

"You already sound like a married couple," Ashley said.

"Nope, not going to happen," Stephanie said.

156

"What's not going to happen?" Ava came out with a tray of lemonade, followed by the rest.

"Nothing. Nothing's going to happen, right Josh?"

"Right."

"It's much too nice a night to stay inside. We thought we would join you," Ava placed the tray down on a table. "Lemonade?"

Her dad handed Josh a beer.

"We were just thinking about a round of badminton, right Ashley?" Josh said.

Badminton sounded like the perfect escape. "Sure, you set it up and I'll be right down." She started upstairs to get her tennis shoes then thought better of it. What better way to play badminton than in bare feet? She knew she was taking a chance, but what was life if you didn't take chances now and then? A life half-lived.

She joined them in the yard below, slipped off her sandals and allowed the cool grass to bless her feet, relishing the feel of solid ground. Like yoga in Central Park, only the grass was longer, lusher, and there were no annoying hordes of tourists. Yes, this was what she needed.

No more talk tonight.

Chapter 29

The day of the rehearsal and rehearsal dinner. This would be her last morning to work-out until she got back to New York. She hurried out the door with hardly a goodbye.

"I'm going over to Grace's this afternoon to help set up for the rehearsal dinner if you want to join me," Ava called to her on her way out.

"Sure. Whatever."

Again, she passed the picture of her mom without stopping. That didn't stop her brain. Jacob getting married. Hard to believe. And to Josie. Her mom had never met Josie. Also hard to believe. It felt like Josie had been part of their family forever, though she and Grace had met when they were nine or ten. What would Mom think about it? What did it matter at this point?

She remembered talking to Jacob about it last night, after Aunt Kathleen and the rest had left, while they watched the sunset from the deck.

"Hard to believe Grace married, and you getting married. What do you think Mom would have thought about this?"

"I'm sure she would be delighted. Abel's a great guy, and Josie … Well, you know Josie."

"I do. Mom would have loved her from the start. That's just the way she was. Hey, um … did Grace tell you about seeing Mom when she was under anesthetic?"

"Yes, she did."

"Don't you find it a little strange?"

"Not really. You know, sometimes, it's like Mom is talking to me. I dream about her sometimes."

"That's a dream. You know that's not real."

Jacob shrugged. "Seems real enough at the time."

"Grace says this was real."

"If Grace says something is real, I believe her. Don't you? Don't you ever talk to Mom?"

"I used to. In high school. But I outgrew it." She took a sip of water. "I wonder why I don't dream about Mom."

"Maybe you aren't open to it."

"Maybe."

"Or maybe because I was always Mom's favorite," Jacob teased.

"Do you want me to pour water on you again?"

"Remember, I give back worse than I get."

She thought about that conversation now, as she stretched. Why didn't Mom come to her the way she did Jacob and Grace? Was she that unreachable? You would think, more than anyone, her mom would visit her. She's the one who followed in her mom's footsteps. Went beyond them, going so much farther than her mom would have imagined.

Maybe Jacob was right. Maybe Mom didn't come to her in her dreams because she wasn't open to it. Maybe that was why her mom left her the poems. That was her mom's way of reaching out to her. Even back then, back in the midst of all of her pain, her mom had been thinking about her, worrying about her.

Ashley didn't believe in spirits. If she were to open herself up to this, what would follow? Would the tapestry that was her life start to unravel?

She stood up and went through her routine. The inside of her head spun as she twirled in a frenzy of pent-up thoughts and exasperation. She stumbled but didn't fall, her timing off. When would she be back in New York where her life was simpler? She couldn't wait. Now she just had to survive the weekend. She laughed at a YouTube video sent by Audra—cat ballet. Then texted her back with multiple emojis.

After her workout she rushed home, grabbed a light snack, and ran upstairs to shower and change her clothes for the wedding rehearsal. She couldn't resist opening the folder again, sitting down on her bed and spreading the contents out. She picked up a poem that caught her eye by someone named Rod Mckuen. At the top was written "Thirty-Five." That was how old her mother had been that final year of her life when her cancer had recurred.

She read the poem through carefully, her fingers tracing along the words. It talked about following birds in the rain. Ashley didn't recognize it. She stopped at the last line.

"But one gray day
I'll follow a funeral out of town on the heels of the birds
disappearing into the rain."

Had her mom known what was coming? Would this be her fate as well, dying too soon? Would she follow in her mother's footsteps not only by being a dancer, but by dying young?

"Ashley, it's time to go to the rehearsal," her stepmother called from downstairs.

"I'll be right down." Ashley shut the folder and tucked it away in her suitcase, lest she lose it amid all the events of the next few days. She glanced at her phone again.

Why hadn't the doctor's office called back?

Chapter 30

Cars were gathering in the church parking lot as Ashley pulled up. She didn't want to drive with anyone else, wanted to be free to come and go as she pleased, not hindered by anyone's whims but her own. Ashley cringed at the thought of going inside the church. When was the last time she had been in a church? She couldn't remember.

Ashley had wondered why Josie and Jacob weren't holding the wedding outside. Seemed more in keeping with Josie's love of the outdoors. At one point Josie and Jacob had thought about having the wedding outside, they had told her when she asked. But outside weddings could be risky. If there wasn't rain or a sudden thunderstorm, there was the possibility of smoldering heat. Josie hadn't wanted to have the wedding in the morning to avoid the heat.

"What would our guests do all day while waiting for the reception?" she had told Jacob.

"Drink," Jacob had responded.

"Exactly. Especially your buddies."

And there was concern about Josie walking over uneven grass. Even with her father's support, Josie didn't want to take the chance she might stumble. It was important to her to walk down the aisle at her wedding, even if she couldn't have the shoes of her dreams. That was the deciding factor Jacob and Josie had told Ashley.

It was a beautiful summer day. Light clouds floated across the sky. Ashley hated to go inside, especially into a church. Would the sky suddenly fill with dark clouds and lightning strike the church upon her entrance? Would she hear a booming voice crying out her name in anger? At least it would make it interesting. Like something out of Faust.

Olivia came running to her as she entered the church. "Will you sit with me?" She pulled on Ashley's hand.

"Of course, sweetie." Ashley looked around the building. Small changes here and there, but overall it was the way she remembered.

"The roof hasn't caved in." Caleb approached her.

"Ha ha. You know, I don't believe in God, or the devil."

"Shame. I haven't seen a good theophany in forever."

"What's a theophany?"

"A showing of God. God coming in power and majesty throwing lightning bolts."

Ashley raised her eyebrows and rolled her eyes.

"But then I've also seen God in an awesome sunrise or my newborn baby's eyes." He looked down at Olivia and ruffled her hair. "We're all right, aren't we? After Wednesday night and all. You're not angry, are you?"

"No, of course not. Why would I be? You only said what we both know."

"That's good, though I did used to like how your eyes flashed lightning bolts when you were angry. You're a theophany on your own. Ashley's righteous anger."

"Why is it all anyone remembers about me is negative?"

"I wouldn't call it negative. You had a will of your own. I like strong women."

"And then they try to cover what they just said by putting a positive spin on it. I'm tired of it. Everybody is so … darn … nice. I'm sick of it."

"Now that's the Ashley I remember. Full of spunk."

"Stop it, Caleb. It's not funny. Why do I have to be the bad girl around all of the saints of Cascade Falls?"

"Hey, no one has said that. Least of all me. I know far too well that I'm not a saint."

"Well, everybody thinks you are, especially my parents. You all are too good for me."

"Whoa. Where is this coming from?"

Ashley shook her head. She didn't know what had gotten into her. She glanced at her phone. Still no message from the doctor's office. That was it. She was just on edge because she hadn't heard anything yet. That was a good excuse for her behavior.

Uncle Joe called everybody to the front of the church.

"Come on, Olivia." Ashley took the girl's hand and led her down the aisle, ignoring Caleb.

There was the required prayer offered by her uncle. "Blah, blah, blah," was all she heard.

"Okay, Josie. You line up your bridal party," Uncle Joe said.

Josie paired them up. First the matron of honor, Grace, with the best man, Alex. Then she was introduced to her partner, Dante Jones, another Golden State Warrior, before pairing Dawn and Andrew.

Ashley looked up at the lean, muscular man. Brown eyes sparkled out of his dark face as he smiled and linked his arm in hers.

"You're the infamous Ashley Reese, prima ballerina."

"You know me?"

"Just what Jacob told me. And what my wife and daughters told me. Seems they saw you dance in *Swan Lake* the time you toured in San Francisco. Your fame precedes you. My wife will never forgive me if I don't introduce you to her." He pointed to the pews where family members of the bridal party were sitting and waved at an attractive woman sitting next to Alex's wife and Josie's parents. The woman smiled and waved at Ashley.

"It appears I have a fan." Ashley did a slight wave back.

"Not just my wife. My daughters. They are determined to be the next Misty Copeland."

"Not interested in basketball?"

"They can do both, can't they?"

"That they can."

"Okay, listen up." Josie's voice echoed in the church, reverberating against the walls.

"Wow. I didn't know she had it in her," Ashley whispered to Dante.

"You should hear her when she's really angry," Dante whispered back.

Josie glared at the two of them.

"I guess she means us." They exchanged a conspiratorial glance and stopped talking.

"Okay. Now that I've got your attention, take over, Pastor." Josie joined her bridesmaids as Uncle Joe sent them to the back of the church. Then he instructed the groomsmen where to stand. Olivia clung to Ashley's hand while they were joined by the other flower girl and the ring bearer.

Josh walked Grandma to her seat with Peter, then Abel escorted Dad and Ava down the aisle. Caleb walked Josie's mom down the aisle while Josie's dad waited with Josie.

Josie squatted down next to the three children. She gave Olivia and Shandra baskets to carry. "There will be rose petals in the baskets tomorrow. I want you to pretend to be throwing out the petals while you walk."

"Rose petals?" Ashley asked. "I thought you were more of a wildflower person."

"Hush," Grace poked her to quiet her.

"You two girls walk together, followed by Brad. Okay?"

"I want Ashley to walk with me."

"Sweetie, I can't. I have to walk by myself before you. You get to go right before your Aunt Josie. You're the most important person here after Aunt Josie."

"No, I want you."

Ashley grimaced at the others and squatted down. What had she done? How had Olivia gone from hating her to this in one short week?' "You know, Olivia, you're older than Shandra and Brad. They're going to need you to help them. You have to set an example for them. Do you think you can do that?"

"No. I want you to walk with me." Her fingers popped back in her mouth.

Ashley looked up at Josie. "How about if I walk down with her just one time to show her what to do?" she asked Josie, then added to Olivia. "Would that help, Olivia?" Ashley gently pulled Olivia's fingers out of her mouth.

Olivia nodded. Ashley walked down the aisle and took her place next to Dawn, then snuck to the back of the church and took Olivia's hand. When Shandra saw her mother, she ran to her so Talia had to come back and take Shandra's hand till all three were in place.

"Can we try that again?" Uncle Joe said after they reached the front. He squatted down in front of the three children. "That was very good. Now, do you think you can do that again, this time by yourself?"

Ashley walked Olivia back to Josie.

"I'm going to be up there with your Aunt Grace," Ashley pointed to the altar where Grace waved at Olivia, then Ashley went to her spot.

With some urging from the people in the pews, the threesome made it down the aisle together. Shandra ran to her mother, Brad to Scott and Alex. Olivia went up and stood next to Ashley. Caleb tried to take her away.

"She's okay with me, right Josie?"

"Tomorrow Chelsea will be here to help with Olivia," Caleb said. "You like Aunt Chelsea, don't you, Olivia?" Olivia popped her fingers back in her mouth without answering.

Josie walked down the aisle with her dad while everyone clapped and whistled.

"Okay, get it out of your system," Josie said. "There'll be none of that tomorrow."

"Think of it like a basketball game," Jacob said. "You can practice all you want, but once the game starts, you never know what might happen. It's part of the beauty of the game."

"I prefer a ballet where everything is choreographed. Right, Ashley?" Josie responded.

Uncle Joe walked them through the rest of the service, then they ran through it one more time with music.

As Dante walked down the aisle with her, he leaned over, "I hear we are supposed to dance together with the rest of the bridal party."

"That's right. A waltz."

"Lame." Dante shook his head. "Can we practice some time tonight?"

"Sure," Ashley assured him. "Don't worry. Remember, you'll be dancing with a prima ballerina."

"I'm no slouch on the dance floor. I've got some moves."

"That's yet to be seen," Ashley smiled, her arm linked in his as they walked together.

Chapter 31

After the rehearsal, all headed over to Grace and Abel's for cocktails and dinner.

"I want to ride with Ashley," Olivia insisted.

"As long as that's okay with Ashley. I've got to pick up Chelsea anyway," Caleb said.

"Chelsea's coming?" Ashley asked.

"She would have been at the rehearsal but couldn't get out of work. Something wrong? She's going to help me with Olivia."

"No, not at all." Ashley took Olivia's hand. "Come on, Olivia." Ashley strapped her into the back seat.

"Daddy says you are going away." Ashley heard the small voice from behind her.

"That's right, Olivia. I'm going back to New York."

"But you'll come back?"

"I will, or you can come see me in New York. Remember, for *The Nutcracker Ballet* and then the Christmas tree in Rockefeller Plaza."

"And the zoo."

"That's right."

Olivia ran off to play with the other kids while Ashley joined the adults for cocktails. "Who's watching the kids?"

"Gus and Caroline. That way the parents can have a break."

Ashley was relieved. This helping with a five-year-old was harder than she had imagined, much as she loved Olivia. How did Caleb do it? But then what choice did he have? You do what you have to do.

Ashley checked her phone again. No message. She knew it was getting late, the office would be closed soon. She called and left another message. "This is Ashley Reese. I'm still waiting on the results of my biopsy." Then Ashley went to the bar.

"I'll have a martini," she told the bartender. "A stiff one." Would this day ever by over?

She looked into the room that was set up for dinner. Somehow Ava had everything set up to fit over thirty adults without feeling crowded. The kids were outside, playing. They were going to have picnic food.

A catered buffet was set up on the patio, with drinks on the side.

"I thought you were going to barbecue?" Ashley asked Abel as she examined the set up.

"That was my thought too, but Grace vetoed that when she realized how many guests we were going to have."

"Smart woman."

"That's why I married her."

"You talking about me?" Grace slipped up beside Abel.

"Always." He leaned over, kissed her, and rubbed her belly.

"I could use your help getting the adults into the dining area."

"Anything for you."

Other guests drifted in. There was all her family, including cousins and their kids, Josie's family, plus the bridal party and their families.

"Where's this Michael you told us about?" Stephanie joined her.

"He should be here any time now." She checked her phone again. There was a text from Michael, nothing from the doctor. What was the hold-up? But then bad news could wait, couldn't it? It wasn't going away, wouldn't change for her wanting it to.

"Plane landed. Will be there soon." She read Michael's text. Depending on the traffic, that would take anywhere from one hour to three. Nothing like rush hour traffic out of Detroit on a Friday afternoon. But Michael was used to New York traffic. This would be nothing to him.

"You're brave. Introducing him to the whole family at once like this. You sure he won't go running back to New York?"

"Michael doesn't run away from anybody or anything," Ashley replied, but inside she was asking herself the same question. Why had she insisted on him coming? Sure, he had to meet her family sometime, but all at once like this? Maybe it would have been better to introduce him gradually. A long weekend when nothing was going on. Then maybe Christmas. Oh, wait. That's right. She was always tied up with *The Nutcracker* over Christmas. She went for another martini.

Caleb arrived with Chelsea as Grace corralled all her guests into the large room where they had made table decorations last week. Ava had worked her magic again, turning the utility room into a banquet hall.

Ashley sat at a table with her parents, Josie's parents, Grace and Abel, and Abel's grandfather. Jacob and Josie sat with the rest of the bridal party and their spouses/significant others. Other guests spread out in the room. Ashley saw Caleb come in with Chelsea and sit at a table with Aunt Kathleen and Uncle Joe and their family.

Ashley's dad stood up once everyone was seated. "As the father of the groom, I'd like to welcome everyone to this dinner in celebration of the pending marriage of my son, Jacob, to his beloved, Josie. We're happy you could join us."

"Hey, Uncle Dale, free food and drinks, nothing could keep us away," Josh joked.

Her father nodded and raised his glass to Josh. "It's tradition that the matron of honor and best man toast the bridal couple at the wedding reception, so I thought I would take this opportunity to toast my son and my soon-to-be daughter.

"Jacob, I'm so proud of the man you've become. Who would have thought that prankster who was constantly in trouble during high school would not only play in the NBA, but capture the heart of an incredible woman? Josie, I love you like a daughter already. Our family wouldn't be complete without you." Her dad raised his glass higher, looking about the room. "Welcome to the family. May God bless you with many years together." All raised their glasses and drank. Ashley switched from martinis to champagne. Martinis went down far too easy.

Her dad then invited other guests to stand and share memories and prayers for the couple. Ashley began to feel light-headed as this went on. She glanced down at her phone. Another text message from Michael. "In Ann Arbor. There soon." She stood up to get a breath of fresh air and some appetizers to soak up the alcohol.

"Ashley. What do you want to say to your brother and his bride to be?" Her dad stopped her before she could leave the table.

What could she say? What did she want to say? That she wanted out of here. But that wouldn't go over well. She took a deep breath and raised her glass.

"It's been a long time since I left Cascade Falls. A long time since I've been home. And I can't help but think of my mom—our mom, Jacob and Grace. She was and will always be my inspiration. I loved her so much. And I love you, too, Dad, Ava. All of you, my family. That includes you, Josie." Why was the floor moving?

"I remember how, twenty-seven years ago, when my mom was around my age, how she found a lump in her breast that was cancer and led to her death. I don't know how to say this. I've been keeping it from all of you …"

Ava reached for Ashley's hand, shaking her head to stop her. Ashley squeezed her stepmom's hand before continuing.

"I don't know how else to say it but to say it …

"Ashley —" Ava whispered. "Don't." Ashley ignored her.

"There's a lump in my breast, just like my mom. I don't have the results of the biopsy yet, but …" Her phone chirped. Ashley saw it was from the doctor's office. "Wait. I have to take this. There's a message from the doctor." She opened the message, read it, blinked then read it again. Was it correct? Couldn't be. "It's benign," Ashley whispered.

"What did you say, Ashley?" Aunt Kathleen spoke up in the hushed room.

"It's benign. No cancer." She held up her phone. It seemed anticlimactic after her build-up. She had been so sure it was going to be positive for cancer.

"That's good." Aunt Kathleen led the chorus of stunted congratulations.

Ashley looked at the door. There was Michael, standing in the doorway. How long had he been there? How much had he heard? Well, time to come clean with everyone. No more secrets. "And this handsome man," she waved her hand in his direction, "is Michael, my fiancé."

Everyone's eyes turned to the door as Michael did a small wave to everyone, looking out of his element. Ashley had never known him to be out of his element.

"Congratulations," again was heard in the room followed by applause and murmurs of surprise. Ava got up and gave Michael a hug then guided him to their table.

"Oh, and here's to my brother Jacob and my sister-to-be, Josie," Ashley added as an afterthought. Now she really needed some food. She sat down as her head swirled.

Michael sat down next to her. "What was that about?"

"I'll explain later. Could you get me something to eat? There's appetizers on the patio. Some cheese and crackers and veggies."

"I'll get it," Abel told her, putting his hand on Michael's shoulder.

"Way to make Jacob's wedding all about you," Grace said before standing up and asking Uncle Joe to bless the food. Ashley looked down at her hands. Would this day ever be over? Where was that plate of food?

Uncle Joe started to pray. "Heavenly Father, you know us better than we know ourselves. You know what we need. We pray that you might give us what we need each and every day. We thank you for good news, new friends and for family. We ask that you bless Jacob and Josie on this their wedding eve. Keep them always in your love. Bless the food we are about to share, and all gathered here. Amen."

Ashley heard the words through a fog, but she heard them rather than the blah, blah, blah, she usually heard whenever anyone prayed. How can God, who wasn't real, know what she needed when she didn't know herself? Good news though. She should be happy. Cancer free and now everyone knew about Michael. No more holding back. Why didn't she feel better? Maybe it hadn't been the best way to tell everyone, but at least it was out.

She gave a crooked smile to Michael. How much had he heard?

"You had a biopsy for possible cancer, and you didn't tell me? That's something we are supposed to share," he whispered.

Oops. He had heard. "I didn't know about it till I was here. I didn't want to tell you over the phone. It all happened so fast."

Abel put a small plate with the veggies, cheese, and crackers she had requested in front of her. She ate the crackers first, allowing the carbs to soak up the swishing in her stomach.

"How much have you had to drink?" Michael asked.

Clearly not enough. She could still feel. "Not that much. A martini or two, two glasses of champagne. I haven't had much to eat today."

"Like most days."

Ashley knew this wasn't over but was happy when everyone at her table got up to get their meals. "Would you bring me a plate, Michael? You know what I like."

The sound of conversation filled the room. Ashley was relieved to hear people talk about something besides her. They all had their own lives to live, their own challenges and small blessings to talk about.

Her dad, Ava, and Abel took care of Michael, making sure he felt welcome and had everything he needed. All the things she should have been doing if she wasn't so intoxicated. Ashley finished off the small plate and headed outside for some fresh air, not waiting for the dinner plate Michael was preparing. She avoided the play area filled with children lest Olivia latch onto her, instead walking to where she could see the horses being rounded up and put into the barn.

"You're a piece of work," a deep voice sounded alongside of her. Dante. Sitting on the grassy slope.

"What are you doing out here?"

"I might say the same, but I heard your speech. I'd want to hide too if I had said that."

"Was it really that bad?"

"Worse."

"I better apologize."

"Why? So you can feel better?"

"Because that's what you do when you do something wrong. To let Jacob and Josie know how bad I feel about it," Ashley stammered.

"To make you feel better," Dante stated. "Sit down." Dante patted the grass next to him. "Now what was that all about? You're telling me you couldn't come up with a better place to tell everyone about a health scare than your brother's rehearsal dinner?"

"When you put it that way …" Ashley eased herself on to the grass.

"There's no other way to put it."

"I've kept it secret all this time. I didn't want to spoil Jacob's wedding, but then, I guess I couldn't keep it in anymore."

"You've been carrying the secret for how long? Two weeks? Or less? You couldn't keep it for two more days?"

"Less," Ashley mumbled. "I didn't mean for it to come out like that."

"Look, Ashley. I deal with a lot of egos, on and off the court. I have a big ego myself, so I know how easy it is to lie to yourself."

"I'm not lying."

"You keep telling yourself that. All I know is that until you get right with your God, nothing else will be right in your life."

Where was that coming from? Even in her alcohol induced fog that was off-base. "What do you know about me? You know I don't believe in God?" Ashley's eyes flared.

"Jacob said some such nonsense. I planned to see for myself. How can someone so smart be so foolish?" He shook his head. Ashley strained to see his face in the dimming light.

"It's not foolishness. You say until I get right with God my life won't be right? What do you know about my life? I've made it, all on my own. No help from your God."

"If that's what you believe."

"It's what I know." Ashley would have jumped up and left, but the ground was whirling.

"You think you did it on your own, but I know, no one does anything in this world on their own, except maybe when you mess up your life. You get all the credit for that. You may not believe it, but God has been in your life in ways you never imagined."

"That's what I hate about you Jesus freaks. You're so certain you're right. You don't allow for anyone else's point of view. It's so arrogant."

"Arrogant?" Dante paused and shrugged. "Or true humility? Humility that recognizes everything I have comes from God. All my blessings, my successes, my family. My failures are my own. Life lessons. Arrogance is believing you've achieved everything on your own."

"Maybe your successes come from your God, but mine I earned on my own by hard work." Ashley started to stand up despite the weakness in her knees. At least the ground was no longer moving.

"Wait. Don't go." He rested his hand on her arm. "Sorry. I didn't mean for this to turn into an argument. We do have to dance together tomorrow."

"Right. The waltz." The last thing she wanted was to dance with him tomorrow or any time. What she wanted was to get away, try to clear her head, if that was possible.

"All I wanted to say, was," his voice softened, "until you get right with God, nothing will really be right. It might appear to be right, but it won't be. That's all. I said it. I won't say anything else. Okay?"

Ashley didn't believe him. Still, she had to dance with him tomorrow.

"Okay. As long as you don't say anything more about your God. Otherwise, I'm leaving, dance or no dance." Ashley settled back down. She wasn't sure she was steady enough on her feet to get up anyway.

"Now, about this dance."

"What about it?" Ashley asked.

"Nothing, but don't you think a waltz is pretty lame, especially when you have two such talented dancers?"

"I'm listening." Ashley was intrigued. She wondered what Dante had in mind. It helped take her mind off the mess she had created that was waiting for her to clean it up.

Ashley sat back down on the grass when Dante went inside after working out their dance for the wedding reception tomorrow night.

"Dante said I would find you out here." It was Michael.

"Oh, you met him."

"And your parents, your brother and sister, aunt and uncles, Grandma and a whole host of other relatives and friends."

"Sorry. Pretty overwhelming."

Michael sat down next to her. "Nothing like hearing your fiancé announce to the world that she might have breast cancer before she tells you."

"That was bad, wasn't it?" Ashley grimaced.

"Yes, but … so like you. I hate to say it. You always have a flair for the dramatic. It's one of the many things I love about you, though it doesn't always make it easy."

"I'm sorry."

"Why didn't you tell your parents we were engaged? You had ten days to tell them. Surely my name came up now and then?"

"I tried to, but it never seemed like the right time."

"Because you wanted to have the greatest impact. What better time to tell everyone than at your brother's rehearsal dinner? Wait — I take that back. You could have had an even greater impact if you had waited till the wedding reception. Or better yet, the wedding." His tone was teasing but he made his point, like he usually did.

"See, it could have been worse."

"My crazy ballerina. Life with you is definitely not dull." Michael put his arm around her and hugged her as they watched the sun sink lower into the red sky.

"What do we do now?" Ashley snuggled into his arm where it was safe and uncomplicated. Michael knew her better than she realized.

"You, my dear, need to go back into that room and face your family."

Ashley frowned. "What are you going to do?"

"I'm going to get my suitcase out of my car. Your family is wonderful, especially your parents and Abel, your brother-in-law. Abel insisted I stay with him and Grace."

"I thought you brought work with you."

"I did. Abel has plenty of room for me to set up my laptop and get my work done before the wedding."

Ashley walked back into the room where dinner had been served while Michael went out to his rental car. Most of the guests were already done eating. The plate Michael had prepared for her was cold. Just as well. She ate the salad and vegetables and threw out the rest.

The caterers were busy cleaning up as guests milled about until Grace announced it was time to decorate the church hall for tomorrow. Parents rounded up children and got them home to bed. Ashley didn't get to say a word to Caleb before he left with Chelsea, Olivia over his shoulder. Just as well.

Michael came back from the room Abel had assigned him, his clothes changed.

"Where are you going?" Ashley asked.

"With you, to the church to decorate. I want to experience everything about what a wedding in Cascade Falls is like. Besides, it's not every day one gets to hang out with two Golden State Warriors."

Michael climbed into the passenger seat of her car. Yes, he was about to experience life in Cascade Falls in general, her family in particular.

Chapter 32

When Ashley and Michael arrived, the other members of the bridal party were already at work, transforming the church hall into an appropriate venue for a wedding. Michael helped Abel and the groomsmen set up and arrange tables and chairs while Ashley and the bridesmaids worked on seating arrangements, setting up a table in the entryway with place cards and table assignments. Michael was back in his element. He had a way of fitting in—something she wasn't good at.

After the tables were covered with tablecloths and decorated, Ashley sat down with Jacob and Grace as they assessed what remained to be done.

"Where's Josie?" Ashley asked.

"I sent her home to rest," Jacob said.

"I wanted to apologize to both of you for what I said at dinner tonight."

"Why apologize? You were just being you," Jacob said. Grace's face was strained, like she was holding something back, or getting ready to pounce. Ashley brushed it off and focused on her brother.

"But this is supposed to be your big day. I didn't mean to take away from that."

"Ashley, I meant what I said about this being a basketball game. You might plan one thing, but where people are involved, you never know what will happen. It's what keeps the game interesting. What keeps life interesting."

"So, you aren't angry at me?"

"No more than I am for you staying out of our lives for so long. I know you're busy. I am too. But that's no excuse for cutting us out of your life."

"Sorry, Jacob," Ashley muttered.

"It's okay, sis." He hugged her. "But the next time you have a health scare, don't wait until someone's wedding to tell us about it. We'll be there for you."

"You're not getting off so easy," Grace stated. The words she had been holding back started pouring forth. "You always have to be the center of attention. Well, you don't get to have that this weekend. This is Josie's wedding and if you won't fight for it …," Grace looked at Jacob, "then I will. You don't upstage my best friend and walk away with just an apology."

Upstage her? Was that what she had done? Seems she had done it so many times in her career she no longer realized it when she did. "I'm sorry, Grace. I guess I didn't realize …"

"Oh, you realized. You come home like the prodigal daughter and everyone is so nice to you. You are forgiven for ten years of neglect. And now you try to turn Josie's wedding into your own showcase. It's not going to happen. And if it does, I'll never forgive you. Jacob might. Josie might, because that's how she is. But I won't. Not ever."

Was this really her sister Grace talking? Her sweet sister who was always kind to everyone? Who never had a bad word to say about anyone? If Grace couldn't forgive her, she really must be a monster.

"Grace, I didn't know you felt this way."

"Because all you ever care about is yourself. And everyone goes along with you, because, after all, you're Ashley. You were a prima ballerina long before you earned the title."

"Is this how you really feel?"

"Yes, and the others would agree with me if they had the courage to stand up to you for once." Grace's eyes blazed.

"What's going on?" Abel came up next to Grace and put his arm around her, followed by Michael.

"Just that Grace has finally told me the truth that no one else has the nerve to say. You talk about me keeping secrets. What about this secret? I've always known you resented me. Everybody trying to be so kind and welcoming while inside you resent me, resent my success." Ashley could give as good as she got.

"No, Ashley. That's not what I meant. I don't know what came over me." Grace paused, her eyes no longer blazing. "It's just that you sail through life, never thinking about anyone but yourself. I'm the one who sees how it hurts the ones you claim you love. Our parents. What would it hurt for you to take a minute now and then to call Dad? Just pick up the phone. Dad won't say so, but it would mean the world to him to hear from you now and then."

"Jacob, is this how you feel?" Ashley turned to face her brother.

"Maybe not as strong as Grace, but yes. It would be good to hear from you more than every ten years."

"Am I that self-centered?" Ashley looked around the group that had gathered. All heads nodded in agreement, even Dante whom she had just met.

"Dawn, Andrew. You hardly know me. And yet you think I'm self-centered."

"It can come with the territory," Michael said. "Being a prima. But it's not all you are."

"We love you anyway, Ashley," Jacob said.

"Despite me being a self-centered shrew," Ashley said. "Michael, do you still have a room reserved?"

"Sorry, love. I cancelled it when Abel offered me a place to stay."

"I don't know where I'll stay, but if that's how you feel, I don't see how I can stay with any of you."

"Ashley …" Grace started.

"Don't worry. I won't bail on the wedding. I'm a professional. The show must go on. Don't expect me to stay around any longer than I have to. Michael, let's go." Ashley stood up.

"Ashley, my stuff's at Grace and Abel's. Where are you going?"

"Anywhere but here."

"Don't be melodramatic, Ashley." Michael gently placed his hand on her arm to soften his words.

"Is that what I'm doing?"

"Yes, dear. It might work in a play, but not in real life." Ashley knew what he was doing. He was trying to save her from herself as he had done other times before, helping her to temper her outburst, but she wouldn't listen to him. Not this time.

"Very well then. It's time for me to leave."

Ashley left Michael with her family and started to drive. But where to? She had nowhere to go. Even if she got a room at a hotel, she didn't have a change of clothing. She had no choice but to go home. She would put on an act, make it through the weekend, then she would never come back.

But there was one person she could call.

Chapter 33

Ashley waited in her car while the phone rang. She was about to hang up when a sleepy voice answered, "Hello?"

"Caleb."

"Ashley?"

"Caleb, am I a terrible person?"

"What? What are you talking about?"

"Am I a bad person?"

"Ashley, what is this about? If it's about what you said tonight, no. Maybe a little rash, but that doesn't make you a bad person."

"Grace said I was a terrible person."

"Grace? Your sister Grace? You must have misunderstood. Where are you?"

"In your driveway." Ashley saw the curtains in Caleb's bedroom move. She stepped out of her car and waved at him.

"Okay. I'll be down in a minute."

Ashley paced around her car while she waited, her shoulders uncharacteristically hunched.

"We can sit out back," Caleb said when he joined her.

"What about Olivia?"

"Don't worry. Once she's out, she's out for good. And if not, I have her monitor." Caleb showed her a small monitor with a grey image of a bed loaded with stuffed animals and a mound of blankets that Ashley figured was Olivia.

They went into his backyard and sat together side by side on the top of his picnic table.

"Nice night," Caleb said. "Reminds me of other nights, only you didn't have to sneak out to see me this time and I don't have to worry about my dad catching us, just Olivia."

Ashley sat in silence, staring across the yard into the dark.

"Tell me. What is this about?" He gently squeezed her arm to get her attention.

"Since I've been back, everyone's been so nice to me."

"That's good, isn't it?"

"No, because they've been lying." She didn't have to look at Caleb to know what he was doing, raising his eyebrows and shaking his head as he always did. "You don't believe me, do you?"

"Look, Ashley, who's everyone? Your parents? Jacob? Grace? I've never known any of them to lie."

"It's not an outright lie."

"Then what is it?" Caleb asked.

"It's not telling the whole truth, holding back their true feelings about me."

"Like you held back, not telling us about your cancer scare."

"I guess I deserve that." Ashley sighed. "I always knew that my family hated me for leaving and never coming back. They were just pretending they didn't."

"Who told you that?"

"Grace, well not in so many words, but she might as well. She said I was self-centered and I didn't realize how much I hurt Dad and Ava by not staying in touch."

"That sounds like the truth to me. Your dad, he'd never say it, but don't you think he misses you? That there isn't a day that he doesn't wonder how his Ashley is doing? He loves you too much to hold you back. I don't know Ava as well, but I expect it's the same for her."

"I would think Ava was glad to be rid of me. I always was a nuisance to her. Without me around she could have my dad all to herself." Ashley continued to stare across the dark yard, barely lit by a crescent moon and stars hidden behind clouds.

"Has Ava ever acted that way towards you?"

"No, she's too good."

"I suspect it was more you who wanted her out of your way so you could have your dad to yourself."

"Why do you think that?" She turned to face Caleb.

"Because I see how Olivia acts around women my age that she sees as a threat."

"She's too little to think that." Ashley shook her head. Or was she?

"She may not realize why she acts the way she does. It doesn't change the fact."

"Okay. I didn't want Ava around at first, but after a while I was happy she was there to occupy my dad so he wouldn't overfocus on me."

"So, you had reason to hate Ava when you were little. What reason does Ava, or your dad, have to hate you?"

"Because I've treated them so bad. Grace is right. I've only thought about me all these years. Is it any wonder they hate me?"

"I highly doubt anyone hates you."

"Well, if they don't, they should." She turned away from him.

"Ashley." Caleb interlocked his arm around hers and squeezed her hand. "You've always had a flair for the dramatic."

"That's what others have said. What do they mean?" She looked back at the sliver of moon, partially hidden by clouds, as she asked herself the same question.

"That for you, life is a drama and you're the heroine. Everything revolves around you. Everything is big, larger than life. There are no small events in your life."

"Isn't that the same for everyone? We're all the lead in our own story."

"Maybe when we were teenagers, but eventually we grow up and realize there is more to life than our own small ambitions and schemes."

"Are you saying I'm immature?" She returned her gaze to his face, seeking the answers she was struggling to accept. For some reason, when Caleb implied as much, she wasn't offended.

"I'm saying, in your own way, you haven't taken that step into reality. And why should you? You've gotten everything you worked for. You have a charmed life."

"It wasn't easy."

"I'm sure it wasn't."

"I worked hard. There are things I did to get ahead. I'm not proud of them, Caleb. I'm a terrible person." Again she turned away. How could anyone, even Caleb, put up with her?

"You go from saying you did things you aren't proud of to being a terrible person. That's what people mean when they say you have a flair for the dramatic."

"What other conclusion can I draw?"

"That everyone does things at one time or another that they aren't proud of. It doesn't make them bad. It just makes them human, an ordinary human being."

Ashley shook her head. How could he say that? "There's nothing worse than being ordinary."

"There you go again. What's wrong with being an ordinary human, loved extraordinarily by God."

"Because, first, there is no God. And second, I may be the worst person to ever walk this earth, but I am not ordinary." Ashley wanted to stamp her foot, like Olivia. If only she hadn't been sitting down.

Caleb laughed. "No, Ashley, you are far from ordinary. What are you going to do? It seems I can't convince you that your family doesn't hate you."

"I guess I have no option but to go home and get through this wedding and then never come back."

"I think you have more options than that, at least the part about never coming back. I would miss you terribly if you never came back. And Olivia would miss you, too." He reached his arm around her shoulder.

Ashley leaned her head against his. "Did I tell you? My grandmother gave me a folder of poems my mom had collected."

"No, you didn't."

"One of the poems talked about following a funeral in the rain and disappearing. I think I was afraid that was going to happen to me. That I was going to die just like my mom, disappearing into the rain."

"Everybody dies. None of us is guaranteed another day. But at least it won't happen to you for a while yet."

"I knew I could talk to you." She continued to lean on his shoulder. "You're the one person who stood up to me when we were kids. You didn't just give me my way."

"We did have some pretty good fights, didn't we? I miss that."

"You never lied to me or kept things from me. You challenged me."

"But I also didn't stand in your way."

"That's because you knew you couldn't."

"That, and the fact that I loved you. Much as your dad loves you. Do you think it was easy for him to let you go, send you to New York?"

Ashley sighed and raised her head, pulling away from him. He had her there. "That was easier than living with a brat who throws temper tantrums."

"Maybe so." Caleb looked up at the moon that had come out from behind a cloud, then turned to face her, his face softened by moonlight. "Ashley, so many people love you. Why do you find that so hard to believe? Your parents, your family. All those people at the dinner tonight. They all love you."

"Not Grace."

"Especially Grace. She's angry with you because she loves you so much. Why are you running away from love?"

Running away? Was that what she was doing? "I'm not running away."

"Then why do you find it so hard to accept that the reason everyone is being nice to you is not because you deserve it, but because they love you? Why are you so quick to judge other people's motives and assume they hate you? None of us deserve the love we receive. I didn't deserve Stacey's love for me. It was all grace. When are you going to stop hating yourself and running away from love?" He stared into her eyes with a force she found hard to deny.

"Because I don't deserve love." She turned away.

"And who determines that?"

"I guess I do." She stared down at her hands, avoiding his gaze, avoiding the cold light of the moon.

"Ashley, you deserve all the love this world has to offer. I wish I could make you see that. None of us deserves God's love, but God loves us anyway."

"Dante said until I get right with God, nothing will be right in my life."

"He's a smart man as well as a great basketball player."

But how could she get right with God when she didn't believe he existed?

They sat in silence for a while till Ashley shivered.

"Getting cold?" Caleb wrapped his arm around her again.

"Just a little."

"I met Michael. He seems very nice."

"He is. He's … perfect. Perfect for me. He's so good to me. I don't know why I should be so lucky to have found him."

"I don't think luck had anything to do with it. He's a lucky man, too, to have you. You believe that, don't you?"

"Hey, I'm Ashley Reese, prima ballerina. Who doesn't love me?"

Caleb laughed and squeezed her shoulders. "I meant what I said the other day. I've never stopped loving you, but I also know it's not meant to be. The only problem is, it seems you have charmed my daughter. I guess I didn't see it when I got you two together."

"Didn't see what?"

"I can't bear for her to have another person leave and never come back. I can handle it, but she's just a little girl. You won't do that to her, will you?"

"No. Or to you. We can still be friends. I need friends who will be honest with me."

"You'll always have me, Ashley." Caleb squeezed her again. "We both have a big day tomorrow. You better be heading home."

Caleb walked her to her car. Was she running? And if so, from whom?

Chapter 34

Ava was still up when she got home.

"What are you doing up? You need your rest," Ashley said.

"Waiting for you. Jacob called and told me what happened. He wanted to make sure you made it home all right. Grace called too. She was worried. I was beginning to think I needed to call for a search party."

"Where's Jacob now?"

"I sent him to bed once he got home."

"And Dad?"

"I didn't tell him. I got to the phone before he did. I told him to go back to sleep. He rolled over and did just that while I went downstairs to take the call. I can worry enough for both of us. Where did you go?"

"To Caleb's. I just needed to talk to someone."

"Ashley, I hope you aren't angry with Grace. She's been working so hard, not just at the Vet clinic, but on this wedding. She wanted everything to be perfect for Josie. And then, being pregnant …"

"I'm not angry with Grace. She only said what everyone was thinking."

"What kind of nonsense is that?"

"You all think I'm a spoiled brat. You're just too nice to say so."

Ava stared at her in disbelief. … Then she opened her mouth. "Okay. You want to hear what I think, Ashley? You are a spoiled brat. You think only of yourself. But that doesn't change the fact that we love you, your father and I. Maybe someday you'll realize that, but for now, there's a wedding to celebrate. There will be no tantrums, no displays. This is your brother's day and I won't have you spoiling it for him, or for any of us. Especially not your father.

"One of these days you're going to realize just how blessed you are to have him as your father, to be part of this family. Until then, you will play the part of beloved daughter and devoted sister. And maybe someday you will realize it is true, that you love us as much as we love you. For now, I'm going to bed. It's going to be a long day for both of us." Ava turned without another word and left Ashley alone.

Ashley sat down at the kitchen table, her mouth hanging open. Ava had never spoken to her like that. Ava had never spoken to anyone like that. Like Grace had never spoken to anyone the way she had talked to her that night. She shook her head.

Weddings sure bring out the worst in people, she thought, as she made her way upstairs.

Chapter 35

It felt like she had just fallen asleep when the alarm went off. She took a quick shower and packed her clothes for the day. They were going to get dressed at the church. She wasn't sure there would be time to stop home and get her dress between getting her hair done and when she needed to be at the church. She pulled out her jewelry, putting the earrings and necklace she had brought for the wedding in with her sandals and other accessories. She paused at the sight of the class ring in the corner, pulled it out, rubbed it in her hand, then placed it inside her clutch purse.

She was at the hairdresser by nine. They were getting mani-pedis and their hair and make-up done. A continental breakfast of fruit, bagels, streusel, and other pastries awaited her, along with coffee, tea, and mimosas. Ashley looked at the mimosa. Remembering what happened last night, she hesitated. Her head said no, but her hand reached for one.

Grace was already there. She took Ashley aside "Ashley, I'm so sorry about what I said last night. I don't know what got into me."

"It's okay, Grace. You're just looking out for your best friend the way you always did."

"But I shouldn't have been so hard on you. You can't help being yourself."

Why do people keep saying that? "No, maybe it's time people start being hard on me."

"I think I'm worried … we're all worried that if we are hard on you, you'll never come back. None of us want that."

Ashley looked in her sister's eyes and realized she meant it. Her sister really did love her, despite how Ashley treated her. And she loved her sister. "I don't want it either, little sister." She hugged Grace and both started crying.

"Hey, save some of that for the wedding." Dawn reached for a mimosa. "To us!"

Ashley found herself next to Josie while getting their pedicures. There were scars on her feet from the many surgeries Josie had had while in college. Ashley knew something about foot pain. She couldn't imagine what Josie had gone through.

Josie saw her looking at the scars. "Just because I can't wear sandals doesn't mean I can't have pretty feet." She smiled and wiggled her toes. "What was that about between you and Grace?"

"Nothing. Family stuff. But I did want to apologize for what I said at dinner last night. It was totally inappropriate. This is supposed to be your day, and instead I was making it all about me. That's what Grace and I were talking about. But it won't happen again. Today is all about you. You are to be the center of everyone's attention."

"Ashley …" Josie shook her head. "I'm marrying a Golden State Warrior. Another Warrior is in the bridal party and three more will be attending the ceremony. Did you ever think this was going to be about me? Or that I would be the center of attention? I resigned myself to the sidelines the minute I started dating your brother. I don't mind. Not everyone has to be center stage. I don't like being the center of attention. I prefer the sidelines."

"Even for your wedding?"

"Even for my wedding. So just relax, forget about it, and enjoy yourself. All that I care about is that at the end of the day, I'll be married to your brother. All this other stuff," Josie waved her hand about the room. "It's fun, but it doesn't matter. We're just glad that you're here."

They spent all morning and into the afternoon at the hairdresser. Then Josie went home to rest before the wedding. Everyone had to be at the church at two o'clock to get dressed and take pictures before the wedding at four.

Ashley took advantage of the break to call Michael. "Have you finished your work?"

"Almost. I wasn't sure you were still talking to me after how you left last night."

"Nonsense. Just family stuff."

"Everything is okay now? You and Grace okay?"

"Yes. We talked this morning. We're sisters. We fight and we make up."

"If you say so. When will I see you?"

"Be at the church by three. I don't know when I'll be free. We're going to be taking pictures, but I'll try to break away before the service. If not …"

"I know. At least I know some people. I'll be sitting with your parents."

Good, Ashley thought. That will take care of Michael. Then she contacted Dante to see if there was time for them to practice their dance.

Josie had been right about her not being the center of attention. When Ashley arrived at the church, news cameras and paparazzi were already waiting, hoping to catch a glimpse of the famous basketball players in attendance. Another good reason for not holding an outdoor wedding where drones could capture pictures and videos. Jacob had hired a videographer to record the ceremony. No news cameras would be allowed in the church. Members of the police department were stationed outside of the wedding to keep intruders out.

From two o'clock on was non-stop. The bridal party dressed in the women's lounge in the church hall. The photographer was in and out taking pictures of them and the groomsmen. They waited downstairs for most of the guests to be seated before they came upstairs and gathered in the foyer. She barely had time to say hello to Michael.

"How are you doing?" Caleb came up beside her.

"I'm good. Really good." She looked over at Grace to let Caleb know she had patched things up with her sister.

The church was filled with friends and extended family. Gwen, the associate pastor, was assisting at the service. Chloe, from the dance studio, was there with her husband, Officer Nash, along with Gwen's husband, another member of the police department, Liam Kelly. People she remembered from church and school, and many others she didn't. Nearly two hundred guests had been invited. Everyone wanted to see the town celebrity, Jacob Reese, get married. Crowds of well-wishers who hadn't been invited to the wedding gathered outside to see the Warriors. Jacob would have invited them all inside, if not for lack of space. He loved to do things in a big way. This was Jacob's dream, not Josie's, as Josie had told her this morning.

"I get the honeymoon I want, so Jacob gets the big wedding he wants. It's only fair."

The service went smoothly. The two flower girls successfully made it down the aisle with no mishaps. It was Brad who decided to not cooperate, sitting down in the middle of the aisle until his dad had to carry him down the rest of the way. It all made for good theater. These things you can't plan. They happen spontaneously. Ashley didn't even mind all the prayers that much. Sometimes she even listened. She smiled and did a quick wave to Michael once in place at the altar. What was he thinking about all of this?

After the service, they rode around town in the limo. Even though the reception was in the church hall, Jacob had insisted on a limo for the bridal party so they could drive through Cascade Falls in style before the reception.

This time when the toasts were made, there were no mistakes. Grace started them off.

"Josie, you've been my friend since we were in fifth grade, playing fairy princess and making up adventures. Never did I think back then that someday your prince would come in the form of my brother, Jacob. You've been like a sister to me all these years, and now I'm so glad that Jacob is making it formal by marrying you. Jacob, Josie — I love you both. The adventure is just beginning."

Alex then offered his toast. "Jacob, what can I say? You've been a brother to me, man, on the court and off during high school. And when an accident ended my career, you continued to be my main support, bringing me along on your dream of playing ball professionally."

"I wouldn't have made it without you," Jacob said.

"Right back at you, brother. You always came out on top, never more than when you finally got the entrancing Josie to agree to marry you. I don't know how you did it, buddy. I've seen you without Josie, and I've seen you with her, and I know you are a much better person for having her in your life. Here's to Jacob, my best friend, and to the best thing that came along in his life, Josie. May God bless you with many happy years together."

Everyone clapped then clinked their glasses until Josie and Jacob kissed.

After dinner, the DJ called the bride and groom onto the dance floor. Jacob and Josie swayed lightly to "What a Wonderful World." Josie even managed a slow twirl. Halfway through the song, the DJ called up Ava, the groom's mother to dance with Jacob, and the bride's father to dance with Josie.

When they sat down, the bridal party came forward. Dante was not a shabby dancer, even within the confines of a waltz. As the music was coming to an end, it abruptly changed from a slow waltz to a fast hip hop.

"This is for you, my man, Jacob, and his lady, Josie," Dante pointed at the bride and groom and shouted. Ashley and Dante took over the dance floor. Under Dante's guidance, Ashley did moves she had never done before. The rest of the bridal party stepped aside as the two cut loose, hopping up and down, breakdancing in their formal attire. It reminded Ashley of singing with Caleb years ago, in high school, when they had played guitars and screamed at the top of their lungs at each other. It was a release, compared with the discipline of ballet. She found herself laughing with abandon, something she rarely did, especially not while dancing ballet.

Applause broke out as they took a bow, then invited everyone to join them on the dance floor.

"That was to get the party going," Dante told Jacob and Josie when they went back to the bridal table. "Now, if you'll excuse me, I'm going to dance with my wife."

Done with her bridesmaid duties for now, Ashley looked for Michael. She found him chatting with Kevin and the other Golden State Warriors who had come for the wedding

"Having a good time?"

"The best. Cascade Falls knows how to throw a party."

"That would be the Reese family that knows how to throw a party." Ashley led him out on the dance floor for a slow dance. "I'm sorry I haven't been able to spend any time with you. Are you glad you came?"

"Ashley, I got to meet your family and the Warriors. It's been great. And now I know more about you."

"You say that like it's a good thing."

"It is, dear. It is." He held her close. "Oh, and my grandfather is almost on board for your fundraisers."

"Both of them?"

"He checked out both dance studios. All it takes now is for his favorite prima to close the deal."

She closed her eyes and just breathed.

Ashley went outside for some fresh air after a few dances. Caleb was standing outside.

"Where's Olivia?"

"Chelsea took her home. We got a babysitter so we could both enjoy the reception. She'll be back as soon as Olivia is set for the night."

"I wanted to thank you for last night. I appreciate it."

"Any time, though before midnight would be preferable."

"I also wanted to give you this." Ashley pulled his class ring out of her clutch purse.

"I wanted you to have it."

"And I'm grateful that I had it for all these years. But now," Ashley added while putting the ring in his hand, "it's time to move on. For both of us. I've got Michael and you've got Chelsea. We both need to be free."

"Hey, Chelsea and I …"

"I know, but if not Chelsea, someone else."

Caleb rolled the ring in his hand. "This doesn't mean you're off the hook for calling now and then. If not me, at least Olivia."

"No, I'm not off the hook. And you still have to bring Olivia to New York in December. Deal?"

"Deal." Caleb continued to roll the ring around in his hand. "You know, I never really saw it ending like this. You off in New York, marrying someone else. Me, here in Cascade Falls."

"What did you see?"

"I guess I always saw us together at some point. Where didn't matter. But now, I realize, where does makes a difference." Caleb put the ring in his pocket. "I guess I better see if Chelsea's back."

Ashley stayed outside. Something didn't feel quite right.

"Had enough of the party?" Uncle Joe slipped up beside her.

"No, I just needed some fresh air."

"I imagine you've had enough of us, of Cascade Falls. Do you miss New York?"

"I do, though not as much as I thought I would."

"Michael seems like a fine man."

"He is, only …"

"Only what?"

"I'm not sure. Dante told me last night that my life would never be right till I got right with God. Then Caleb told me I was running away from love. Do you think I am?"

"Two wise men." Uncle Joe frowned and crinkled his forehead as he considered what to say. Ashley was familiar with this from the times she had seen him for counseling, back before he had married Aunt Kathleen. "What do you think?"

Ashley laughed. "I should have known you would say that. You always had a way of throwing my questions back at me."

"So, what do you think?"

"I don't know. How can I get right with a God I don't believe in?"

"Good question."

"And if I'm running away from love, why?"

"Another good question."

Ashley frowned as she concentrated on the question. "I don't think it has anything to do with my mom, because I know she loved me. You helped me so much when I was back in school. You helped me process my grief."

"You never completely get over such a loss."

"Yes, but you do get on, and I did. I still miss her, but I'm not running away from love, or searching for her love."

"Then whose love are you running away from?"

Ashley's lower lip pushed up into a pout as she thought. "I don't know. My family?"

"Why would that be?"

"I'm afraid they want to bring me back and keep me here."

"But if that was the case, why did they let you go in the first place?"

"I guess that does makes sense." Ashley sighed and looked away.

"Maybe you are running away from yourself."

"Now why would I do that?" She turned back to face him.

"I don't know. Only you can answer that. There's a quote I came across recently, 'Modern man is condemned to success because without God he has no place to take his failure.'"

"I don't get it. I'm not condemned to success. I made it on my own. It was my choice."

"Maybe that's why you're so driven? Maybe you're running away from the possibility of failure. I can pretty much guarantee you will face failure someday. I don't know anyone who hasn't."

"Then maybe you don't know me so well."

Uncle Joe laughed. "Maybe I don't. I've missed our discussions. You always challenge me. I like that."

Ashley didn't miss these discussions, but she didn't say so. At least she had learned that much from Michael. Tact. Diplomacy.

"Or maybe you're running away from God. You don't want to be caught because it might mean you have to make some changes in your life that you aren't ready to make."

Ashley paused. That did make sense. She hated to admit it, but Uncle Joe usually made sense. "Am I the most terrible person ever?"

"No, you're just human, like everybody else."

Ashley ignored the suggestion she was like everybody else. She knew that wasn't true. "Then why do I feel like I'm so terrible?" Ashley asked.

Uncle Joe smiled. "There's a poem I think you would like. *The Hound of Heaven.* It talks precisely about what you are talking about. Running away from God. I'll text it to you." Uncle Joe took out his phone and sent a link to her via text.

"Hound of Heaven — sounds scary, not comforting. Once the hound catches its prey, isn't the prey torn apart?"

"Read the poem. Decide for yourself."

There's that freedom, free will, Uncle Joe was always talking about. She was free to make her own choices, certainly had over the years. Maybe that was what she feared losing if she accepted there was a God? Her ability to do as she pleased.

"Ashley, Joe," Aunt Kathleen called. "Jacob and Josie are cutting the cake."

"I guess that's my cue," Ashley said. "Time to fulfill my responsibilities as a bridesmaid. Thank you. I'll read it. You know, you aren't half bad, for a minister and all."

Uncle Joe laughed and hugged her. "And you aren't half bad, for an atheist and all."

They walked in together, arm in arm. Ashley rejoined Michael. "Have you had enough yet?"

"Not nearly enough. When are you done?"

"Not till the last guest is gone and the hall cleaned up for church tomorrow. The bride and groom get to leave while the bridal party and family members clean up and take care of the presents."

"Another Cascade Falls tradition?"

"It's a Reese family tradition."

"Then I guess I'm not done either. I'm glad, as long as I'm with you." He leaned in and kissed her. "I don't want to ever be done where you are concerned."

Ashley smiled and kissed him back. So much left undone, unsaid. So much to figure out. And tomorrow she would be gone, back to her rightful place in New York. Cascade Falls would recede into the past like other times.

Chapter 36

It had been a long day and a late night, but Ashley woke up the next morning at her usual time. She hadn't slept well. So many unanswered questions, so many disconnected thoughts running through her brain, haunting her dreams. She was being chased by the hound from heaven, or so she thought in the wee hours of the night when all was dark. When she couldn't sleep, she had checked her messages, gone to the link Uncle Joe had sent, read the short clip about the writer, Francis Thompson, then read the poem.

> *"I fled Him down the nights and down the days*
> *I fled Him down the arches of the years*
> *I fled Him down the labyrinthine ways*
> *Of my own mind ..."*

Was that what she was doing? Fleeing God? Lost in the labyrinth of her mind? She didn't understand but there was a truth present in the words that spoke to her.

> *"All things betray thee who betrayest Me."*
> *"Naught shelters thee who wilt not shelter Me."*
> *"Lo, naught contents thee who content'st not Me."*

Was that another way of saying what Dante had said to her—that until you get right with God, nothing else will be right in life? But what did that look like? What would she have to give up? It wasn't like her life was a disaster. She had a good life, a great life. What more could she want? She wasn't a drug addict like the writer of the poem, Francis Thompson. What was Thompson afraid of? What was she afraid of? That she would have to give up everything she had built for herself? That the life she had created was but a lie, built on a fallacy that there is no God?

(For though I knew His love who followed,
Yet was I sore adread lest having Him,
I should have naught beside)

Thompson knew God's love, yet he ran away from God. She didn't know God's love.

Or did she? Ever since coming home, she had been bathed in love. Love of her parents, love of her brother and sister, love of her friend, Caleb, love of her family, Grandmother, Peter, Aunt Kathleen … They forgave her without being asked, without question. They loved and accepted her, more than she deserved, without restriction or condition. If only they had treated her the way she deserved. Shamed her for her obvious failings. Refused to love her when she acted so mean. She didn't deserve their love. That's why she couldn't accept it. And even Michael. He had seen her at her worse and still loved her. She didn't deserve him either. How could she accept that which she hadn't earned? There was no room for free grace in her life. Everything she had, everything she had accomplished had been through her own effort and determination.

Ashley reached for the folder of her mother's poems, pulling it out of its place in her suitcase where she had neatly placed it to read later, when she had more time. Now was the time.

She sifted through the pages, handwritten, copies of poems her mother had loved. She didn't know her mother loved poetry, but it came as no surprise. Some of them didn't have an author listed. Had her mother written them? Why hadn't she shared them with others? The words were positive, uplifting. Was that how her mother had managed to be so strong and positive while dealing with cancer?

Ashley caressed the pages. Touching them brought her mother back to her. She didn't have the dreams or visions of her mom that Jacob and Grace had, but she had this. Suddenly the scent of cocoa butter filled the room. Her mother. Ashley remembered watching her mom slather the lotion on her cracked feet. At the time she had wondered why anyone in their right mind would want to do something that resulted in so much pain. Now, she rubbed lotion on her own sore feet, though she could afford more expensive brands.

Ashley found a copy of *The Hound of Heaven* mixed among the other poems. She wasn't surprised. It was like her mom. She didn't know how she knew; she just did. Had her mother fled from God too? Her mother who had been such a believer, at least as Ashley remembered her. Had her mother had doubts too? Ashley kissed the piece of paper then went back to bed. She fell asleep, bathed in the smell of cocoa butter, wrapped in her mother's love.

Despite her lack of sleep, she felt rested the next morning. She figured it would catch up with her eventually and she would crash. She always did. At least tonight she would be back in her own bed. Hopefully she wouldn't crash before that. Maybe then she'd be able to catch up on her sleep. But no, tomorrow she had to be back at The Company. Such was the life of a prima ballerina.

Ashley began to pack her bags, scanning the room for any forgotten items. She took a last look at the pair of pointe shoes hanging where she had placed them. Should she leave them there for when she returned or take them with her? She took them down and squeezed them into her suitcase. Certainly, she could find room on the walls of her apartment for them. She glanced at the boxes unopened in the corner. They would have to wait for another time.

"You are going over to Grace's so you can say goodbye to everyone, aren't you?" Ava asked her as Ashley entered the kitchen, her hair wet from her shower.

"Yes, Ava. I'll be over as soon as I finish packing. Michael's there anyway. I'll leave from there for the airport."

"See that you do that," Ava said as she and Dale left.

Members of the bridal party and family were munching bagels, pastries, and fruit when she got there. The traditional continental breakfast. She turned down a mimosa.

"Have to drive to the airport."

She sat next to Michael while Jacob and Josie opened presents and Grace and Dawn wrote down what each was and who it was from. She was being spared this chore because she had to leave by noon.

At eleven thirty she announced she had to leave. This way she had plenty of time for the long goodbyes and hugs that were part of every family goodbye. Jacob and Josie took a break from opening presents to say goodbye. There were the customary hugs and small talk.

"I'll be in touch about those fundraisers," Ashley told Aunt Kathleen as they hugged.

"They're going to happen?"

"I just have to work out some details. I'll contact you about dates."

"Maybe this will require a trip to New York to make plans." Aunt Kathleen squeezed her tight.

"Do that. And make sure you bring Grandma with you." Ashley turned from her aunt and hugged her grandma.

Her dad and Ava followed her and Michael outside to their cars.

"Good to meet you," her dad gave Michael a firm handshake, followed by a hug while Ava hugged her.

"Thank you for being a mom to me and setting me straight," Ashley whispered in her ear. "You call me this week when you find out about that thing," she added as she let go of her stepmom.

"What thing?" her dad asked.

"Just girl talk," Ava said and hugged Michael.

"Don't wait another ten years before coming home again," her dad said as he hugged her. "Your room is always available."

"Yes, Daddy."

"I guess we better go back to the party," Ava said. One more quick hug from both before they went back into the house.

Ashley stepped aside while Michael put his luggage into his rental car. "Too bad we weren't able to return your car here. You sure you can find your way to the airport?"

"I got here from the airport, didn't I? How hard can it be?" Ashley put her luggage in her car when Caleb pulled up with Olivia.

"I'm sorry for intruding, but Olivia insisted on seeing you before you left." He shook Michael's hand then got Olivia out of the car.

"I'll go on ahead," Michael said. "See you at the airport." Michael gave her a quick kiss, then climbed into his car and drove down the street.

"Olivia made you a picture," Caleb said as Olivia became suddenly shy.

Ashley squatted down to be at eye level with the little girl. "Can I see it?" She took the picture. "It looks like a Christmas tree."

"Yes, at Rockefeller Plaza."

"And who's that?" Ashley pointed to a stick figure by the tree.

"That's my mom. She's dancing to *The Nutcracker*."

"And who are these people?"

"That's me and you. We're watching my mom dance."

Ashley's heart leaped into her throat as she held back a sob.

"Olivia. It's beautiful. I'll put it on my refrigerator where I can see it every day and think of you. Thank you." She hugged Olivia tight, not wanting to let go.

"You aren't going to go away and never come back?" Olivia squirmed and pulled out of Ashley's embrace.

"No, I'll come visit you — and remember, you and your dad are coming in December." Ashley hugged the small child again. "I'll call you when I get home if it's not too late. Okay?"

"Okay."

Ashley gave Caleb a crooked smile. "Thank you for bringing her over. I would hate to leave without saying goodbye." Ashley looked back at Olivia. "You know, Olivia, they have left over cake from the wedding inside. You didn't get any last night. Why don't you and your dad go in and have some. I'm sure it will be okay."

"Can we, Daddy?"

"Sure." Caleb gave Ashley a hug. "Thank you for everything."

"I'm the one who should be thanking you." Ashley wiped away a tear.

"You're right about that," Caleb teased. "Let's call it even."

Caleb and Olivia waved as she drove out of the driveway. The drive was mostly uneventful, but even though she turned on the GPS, she still ended up circling the airport three times before she finally made it to the car rental place. She joined Michael on the plane just as they were preparing to take off.

"I was beginning to think you were lost."

"Me too," Ashley said as she buckled in.

Chapter 37

Ashley wiped the stage makeup from her face, leaning in to check in the mirror for any remnants before switching to her regular makeup. How many times now had she danced in *The Nutcracker*? How many times as the Sugar Plum fairy? Hard to keep track. Another Sunday matinee filled with admiring little girls, aspiring dancers, like she had been so many lifetimes ago.

"Knock, knock." A familiar face appeared at her door holding a bouquet of flowers. Michael. "Another great performance." He approached and kissed her cheek.

"You think so? I thought I was a little off in the last number."

"If you were, I didn't notice."

"Maybe because you had your eyes on that new dancer. Who are the flowers for? Your latest conquest?"

"My soon-to-be conquest."

"One who doesn't know your charms yet."

"Precisely. She will though." He excused himself to pursue the young woman.

Ashley smiled. Another success on her path to fame. She had managed to successfully breakup with Michael without losing him as a friend or his grandfather's patronage or her position with The Company.

She had broken up with Michael over dinner that fall at the Rainbow Room, high above Rockefeller Plaza. It didn't make any sense. He was the perfect fiancé. She didn't know when she knew it wasn't going to work out. She just did. She had looked out at the expanse below her and realized it wasn't what she wanted anymore. This sprawling city, the night life, the traffic, the shows, the glamor—none of it held the same attraction as when she first came to New York at age seventeen. She didn't know what she wanted;

she just knew it wasn't this. She thought about Olivia and her promise to take her to see the Christmas tree that December. Ashley took one last look at the engagement ring sparkling on her finger — then took it off.

"When did you know?" she asked Michael as she handed him back her engagement ring, amid the chatter of diners at this, their favorite restaurant.

"Know what?" He looked at the ring and shook his head.

"That it wasn't going to work, you and me."

"That? Is that what this is about?" He continued to hold the ring in his hand, looked at her and gave a small smile. "I think I realized it after I met your family. I recognized that underneath it all, under the stage make-up and the bun, was a small-town Midwestern girl. I think I fell deeper in love with you—the real you—yet I knew it was only a matter of time."

"A matter of time?"

"Before you realized the same thing and returned to Cascade Falls. The glamor and excitement of New York won't keep you happy forever. I wouldn't be able to keep you happy forever." He reached for her hand, newly bereft of the engagement ring and lightly rubbed her fingers.

"I hope we can still be friends." Ashley placed her free hand over his.

"Why wouldn't we be?"

"And I'll still be prima?"

"Darling, that was based on your talent and my grandfather's patronage. It was never tied to our relationship."

"Though it was a plus."

"To me, hopefully to you too." He smiled as he put the ring in his pocket. "But the prima, that was all you. You earned it on your own and it will continue to be yours until you choose to leave, or someone younger comes along."

"You might be right about me and New York, but I'm not ready to leave. Not yet. I'm also not ready to give up my position as prima."

"It's all in your hands."

That was where she liked it.

Somehow, after returning from Cascade Falls, she realized she had changed in significant yet almost imperceptible ways. It wasn't evident at first. She had been happy to be back in New York, until she wasn't. What had seemed important before she went home, was now insignificant. She still loved to dance. In some ways she was better than she had been. The edge was gone. There was a softness that hadn't been there before. She felt more able to focus on her performance, less on keeping her position.

She had found herself drawn back to the folder of poems from her mother. She read them over and over, but especially *The Hound from Heaven*. As she reflected on the words, a dance formed in her brain, waiting to be performed. It was like when she was fifteen and had taken the class Letty had taught on lyrical dance. Then she had danced to one of her mom's favorite songs, "I Can Only Imagine." That had been after their dog Lucky died. Lucky had arrived just when she had needed him most, that year before her mother died. He wasn't the hound from heaven, but he had been heaven-sent. She found herself thinking, maybe there was another life for her, as a choreographer, or an artistic director of her own ballet company, or even her mother's dance company.

She had already held her first fundraiser for her mother's dance company and Letty's dance company, a joint one. She kept it simple, performing in Detroit with young dancers from Freedom House. Afterwards she attended a dinner with patrons, establishing connections for herself among supporters of the companies. Michael's grandfather had helped with seed money.

The next fundraiser would be bigger, bringing in dancers from New York. She planned to premiere the dance that was forming in her head at that one. Her debut as a choreographer. With Michael's grandfather's help, she was setting both companies up for long-term success and financial stability.

Another knock on her dressing room door—the stage manager. "There's someone here wants to see you. Says he knows you. He told me to give you this." He handed her an envelope.

A ring fell out onto the counter. A class ring.

Caleb.

"Send him back." She stood and wrapped a dressing gown around her.

"Ashley!" Olivia came running up and hugged her.

"Was it everything you thought it would be?" Ashley asked the girl.

"More. You were wonderful. Wasn't she wonderful, Daddy?"

"Always." Caleb handed her a bouquet of flowers. He looked about the dressing room then shoved his hands in his winter coat pockets. So different from Michael. Michael was at ease wherever he went. Caleb was out of place in this environment. He ran his hand through his hair. "You ready?"

"Clearly not, but I will be." Ashley put the bouquet in a vase, then slipped behind a screen and changed out of her leotard and into jeans and a sweater. "Better?"

"Better."

Ashley could tell that Caleb was more comfortable with this Ashley than her onstage persona. "You know, it's all me. The ballerina onstage and the girl in blue jeans that you remember."

"If you say so."

"I know so."

Olivia was entertaining herself, sitting in front of Ashley's mirror and playing with the different bottles of make-up. Ashley pulled on her winter coat. "You ready, Olivia?"

The girl jumped up and took her hand.

"Where should we go first?" Ashley asked her.

"Rockefeller Plaza. Remember, you promised."

"That we did." Ashley smiled at Caleb.

"Should we take a taxi?" Caleb asked.

"The subway will be faster. Traffic around Rockefeller Plaza is crazy this time of year."

"It's your city."

"That it is." She smiled as Caleb held the door for her and Olivia.

Ashley and Caleb sat side by side in the subway car while Olivia kneeled on the seat and looked out the window, looking for something besides the dark tunnel.

"I broke up with Michael," she stated, looking down at her hands.

"I know. Your dad told me."

"How are my dad and Ava, and everyone?"

"Good, but you know that. Don't you call every week or so?"

That she did. That was one of the ways she had changed. She had called Ava the week after she was back to find out what had happened at her doctor's appointment.

"No MS?"

"No MS, at least that he could tell. I guess my tiredness was just the normal effects of growing older. Maybe it is time for me to retire. I love teaching, but it is challenging. I could visit you in New York more often then. And get to know my future son-in-law better."

Since then, Ashley had called almost weekly, except for when she was on tour. Her dad and Ava had been among the first ones she told about her break-up.

"I wish I could have been there for the birth of Grace's baby. How is she?" Ashley asked as the subway car continued on its path, bumping and jolting its riders as it stopped and started.

"The baby or Grace?"

"Both."

"What is there to say about babies? They poop, they spit-up and they cry. But she's beautiful."

"Of course, she is. She's my niece after all."

"You wouldn't have anything but a beautiful niece."

"No, I wouldn't. I'll even forgive Grace for not naming her after me since she's named after our grandmother and mother, MaryJoy." They hopped off the subway car and ran up the stairs, each holding one of Olivia's hands. Gripping her hands, they moved along Fifth Avenue through the crowd to Rockefeller Plaza.

"There it is, Olivia." Ashley pointed to the Christmas tree up ahead. Caleb picked her up so she could see it better through the crowd. "What do you think?"

"It's not as big as the one in *The Nutcracker*."

"No, but that's a magical tree," Caleb said.

"This one is magical too. In its own way," Ashley said.

"Really? How? I didn't think you believed in magic," Caleb asked.

"I never said I didn't believe in magic, just God. New York is a magical city."

"As is Cascade Falls if you give it a chance. Just in a different way."

"And, you know, that God thing …" Ashley began.

Olivia squirmed. Caleb put her down but held fast to her hand. "Yes?"

"I've been thinking. I'm willing to admit I could be wrong."

"So, you're going from an atheist to an agnostic?"

"You might say that. Maybe even more. Seems I'm being chased by the Hound from Heaven."

"What does that mean?" Caleb turned and faced her, his eyes wide.

"Just a poem I've been reading." Ashley looked down and shuffled her feet, refusing to meet Caleb's stare. "I'm allowing for the possibility. It's one of the poems in the folder my mom left me."

"What happens when it, or the hound, catches you?"

"I don't know." She raised her eyes and smiled. "He hasn't caught me yet. I put it to music and choreographed some steps for it."

"I'd love to see it." He gazed into her eyes.

"You will someday." She stared back into his. She stood unmoving, afraid to lose the moment.

"Can we get closer, Daddy?" Olivia pulled his hand. "I want to see the tree."

Caleb slowly pulled his eyes away from Ashley's. "Okay, but hold onto our hands. We don't want to lose you in the crowd." Caleb and Ashley bumped along, holding tight to Olivia as they slowly made their way through the crowd until they found a spot where they could watch the skaters with the tree in the backdrop. Olivia leaned against the railing.

Christmas lights showed throughout the plaza as skaters glided by.

"I'm not running away anymore. Not from God, not from myself, not from you." Ashley looked across the plaza to the Christmas tree.

"Me?"

Ashley turned and faced him. "You. You always were there for me, in your own way. Even when I was far away."

"You'd be okay with an ordinary life in an ordinary town with this ordinary man?"

"Nothing would be ordinary as long as you're with me."

Caleb laughed. "That's right. With you, nothing is ordinary. One of the reasons I love you. Oh, and your humility."

She laughed as she gazed across the plaza. Despite its size, it felt closed in and small, amid the tree, the towering buildings and the vast throngs of shoppers and sightseers. She was one with the mass of humanity.

"You know, I'm not quite ready to leave New York. I'd like to finish with the spring season."

"I've already waited fifteen years. What's six months more? I'll wait as long as it takes."

"Closer, Daddy." Olivia pulled on his hand. "I want to get closer to the tree."

Caleb caressed Ashley's face with one hand while holding onto Olivia's hand. He leaned forward and pressed his lips against hers. "It's always been you, Ashley. No one but you."

Ashley leaned into him in response. The sound of the crowds, sounds of the season, all swirled about her, blending with Olivia's chatter. She didn't know what the future held, but she knew it would be fabulous. How could it be anything but? It didn't matter where she was. She was Ashley Reese, prima ballerina.

Note to the reader

Thank you for reading *Prima Ballerina*, the last book in my Dancing through Life Series. If this is the first book in the series that you have read, I hope you'll consider reading the other ones. If you have read all of the books in the series, thank you. I hope you have enjoyed the characters and stories and that they have helped you in your own life.

And if you enjoyed this book, it would delight me if you left a review on Amazon or other sites. In this day of e-marketing, you, the reader, have more influence than you may realize. Your review may make the difference between an author finding readers or remaining unknown.

Thank you in advance for posting a review. If you have any questions or comments on this book or any of my writing, please contact me, patricia@patriciamrobertson.com.

Patricia

Other Novels by Patricia M. Robertson

Dreamweavers – Dream again, wherever you are in your life.

Buying Time – Visit the peace movement during the Cold War era of Ronald Regan, SDI (Strategic Defense Initiative) and MAD (Mutually Assured Destruction).

Land of Deep Waters - Honduras, land of deep waters, a country torn apart by civil unrest, violence and poverty: Is it possible to go back?

Magnificent Failure - Is it possible to start over? Failures in the eyes of the world and their own eyes, Diane and Jake found each other.

Dancing Through Life Series

Dancing on a High Wire – What do you do when life knocks you off balance? Join Sara, Joy and Esther as each seeks to find a "new normal" and regain their balance on this high wire we call life.

Still Dancing - Some phone calls we love, others we hate, like the ones Pastor Joe receives from his daughter's school. Or the one Dale received at work, letting him know his wife, Joy, had fallen and was in route to the hospital by ambulance. Could her cancer be back?

A Slow Waltz - The road to healing from loss is a slow one, sometimes going backward and sideways before going forward. Sometimes the biggest barrier to healing lies within us. Join Dale, Kathleen, Ava and others as they journey to forgiveness and healing.

An Irish Slip Step - Kathleen knew about slipping up. As did Chloe, whose life was knocked off balance by an unplanned pregnancy. And then there was that fiery red-head, Mary Helen, who fell in love with an American soldier. Was it a slip-step or one of life's fortuitous missteps that brought them precisely where they were meant to be?

Delicious Secrets - A church secretary was the last job Marcy would have chosen, but she makes the best of it by entertaining herself with real and imagined secrets about church members, until she stumbles upon a secret she would rather not know. Once known, there was no turning back.

Beautiful Questions - Some questions are so big, they can take a lifetime to answer. They are big enough for you to live in, walk around in them, taste them, touch them, and test them. They are beautiful questions. What are the beautiful questions in your life? Join Gwen and others as they ask beautiful questions.

Lyrical Dance - What do you do when all you've ever known about yourself, what gave your life meaning, is wiped away? How do you get it back?

Freedom Dance - All of her life, Letty has struggled to fit in. There is the middle-class world of her parents, the white middle-class world of her friends, and the poverty-stricken world of her cousins. Will she ever find her place in the world?

Man of the Month – The last place Gwen wanted to do her internship was her home town, Cascade Falls. But her father's heart attack and recuperation required her presence. Even worse, her mother starts the "Man of the Month Club" to find eligible young men for Gwen to date until she finds Mr. Right and settles down in Cascade Falls. Would she ever escape her home town?

Rebound - Jacob was the rebound king, both on the court and off. He got up after being knocked down as if nothing had happened. He picked up and dropped women as quickly as the ball in a basketball game. Until he met the one woman who was impervious to his charms. Had he finally found a love to last a lifetime, only to lose her?

Amazing - All her life, Grace lived in the shadow of her famous brother and sister. But there was a greater shadow on her heart, one left by the death of her mother. What made it worse was that she had caused her mother's death. A family of horses and two handsome brothers help Grace, a young veterinarian, realize just how amazing she is.

About the Author

Patricia M. Robertson is an author, speaker and spiritual director, who is committed to helping individuals find God in their every day experience. She also is author of a companion non-fiction book to *Still Dancing, Walking with Families through the Dying Process*, as well as *Walking with Families through Grief,* a companion to *A Slow Waltz*.

She has written other non-fiction books and writes a weekly blog and monthly newsletter. She has a Doctor of Ministry and over thirty-five years of experience in ministry to families. She currently is enjoying her own love story with her husband, Jack, grown children and grandchildren. For more information about her ministry, go to www.patriciamrobertson.com.

www.ingramcontent.com/pod-product-compliance
Lightning Source LLC
Chambersburg PA
CBHW061206210726
48294CB00006B/1770